Morpho

NewCon Press Novellas

Morpho

Philip Palmer

NewCon Press
England

First published in the UK by NewCon Press
41 Wheatsheaf Road, Alconbury Weston, Cambs, PE28 4LF
April 2019

NCP 176 (limited edition hardback)
NCP 177 (softback)

10 9 8 7 6 5 4 3 2 1

ISBN:

978-1-912950-01-0 (hardback)
978-1-912950-03-4 (softback)

Cover art by Peter Hollinghurst
Cover layout by Ian Whates

Minor Editorial meddling by Ian Whates
Book layout by Storm Constantine

Here are some snippets of rolling news:

There are unconfirmed reports of a terrorist assault in the sleepy Yorkshire town of...

No further news as yet on the suspected terror attack in the town of Hebden Bridge. Locals reported...

The Yorkshire Constabulary has categorically denied rumours of a major terror incident in the sleepy Yorkshire town of...

Internet rumours are flying about damage done to historic buildings in the sleepy Yorkshire town of...

We are now hearing that the two confirmed fatalities in the Yorkshire town of Hebden Bridge were caused by an exploding gas main.

Do not believe what you read about the incident in Hebden Bridge last week. Reliable sources say that for once, the bad guys did not win the day. Let us hope so. And our thoughts are with the two individuals who defied, for the first time in recorded history, the powers that be. Remember:

YOU ARE NOT ALONE.

One

Their kind were familiar with fear. It was like oxygen for them; though they did not need to breathe, and only did so to conceal their true nature.

Jane drove fearfully but fast. She was touching speeds of ninety miles per hour on these narrow country lanes. The car's grey shell was blackly scarred with scratches from the tall flanking hedgerows. The smell of burning rubber was like autumn bonfires wafting across the fields.

The armour-plated Jaguar pursuing them was out of sight, its driver clearly too cautious to replicate such speeds. But it had their scent and could not easily be shaken off.

'There's a left turn in fifty yards, unmarked,' said Billy Franco. She knew this too. He was swallowing and reswallowing the same gobbet of vomit but his voice remained calm.

She took the sharp left turn, then hurtled down a road too narrow for tractors, and swerved with a brutal right on to another unmarked B road which would lead them to the Doncaster by-pass where, they hoped, the heavy traffic and its residue of oily smog would cloak them.

A helicopter throbbed above.

'We're done,' he said.

'No.'

'We have lost.'

'No. Let me – get out.'

'What?'

'Get out of the car. I so instruct you.'

He did not know how to disobey a direct command. So Billy opened the car door and threw himself out.

He hit the tarmac like road kill.

Centuries ago Jane was called Ursula and she was the daughter of a

5

mighty Northumberland lord. And Billy, who was called William then, was nothing but a Geordie serf. But the two of them met and, somehow, sensed that they were kindred spirits. Not like other people. And so their love was born, though not declared; for they knew that any liaison between them would be a defiance of the natural order of things.

Then William died of the plague. Ursula took to her bed and wept for a week. Her parents were distraught and sent for the physician who encouraged them to bleed her. Ursula refused the surgeon's knife and wept until her eyes were red balloons but could not tell anyone that she was mourning the death of a scrawny servant who sang bawdy songs to her and who somehow without words had pledged his undying love.

A week after William was carried away by the plague cart, the twelve-year-old Ursula was composed again and willing to discuss with her mother potential matches to bolster their hold in the North. In her heart, though, Ursula felt her life was over. From this moment on, she resolved, all she would know was duty.

As for William – he spent two days buried in the plague pit before he realised that he was truly alive, and not in Hell. It took him another full day to claw his way out. By this point his boils had burst and his skin was flaming hot. He was unable to breathe because of the mass of corpses around him, and yet his heart still beat.

He reached the top of the mountain of bodies at the dead of night and crawled away for three long miles until he found a river and there he doused himself.

Within two more days his boils had healed and his naked white skin was bitter with cold. He broke into a cottage and stole a jerkin and trews and a pair of boots which did not fit and which he had to discard. He walked on bare feet to Alnwick and was caught stealing another pair of boots and was beaten and left for dead. But that 'dead' too passed quickly enough, and the bloodied boy crawled to the safety of the market square. And there, with a stolen knife, he stole more clothes from a beggar boy, together with boots which fitted him.

For three years he lived in the town and worked as a butcher's boy. William was handy with a knife, and oblivious to the frequent nicks and gashes which were a common consequence of his trade.

At the age of fifteen he was a brawny lad and a bonny one. Any girl might lose her heart to him. He went as 'Will Darke' these days and claimed to have family in Berwick-upon-Tweed. No one enquired much, and Will volunteered little.

On a Sunday in the market square young Ursula Warkworth was

walking with her mother on the eve of her wedding day and sensed him. In a town with thousands of citizens, amidst the shit and refuse and the aroma of baked meats, she knew he was there. And she began to run towards him.

When she found him at his trade, this startled butcher boy, she made him drop his knife, and took him by the hand and pulled him into the open lane and without a trace of shame, she kissed him. He hardly recognised her – she had grown up so much, her fair hair had darkened, and the girl had become a woman. But the moment they kissed, their souls touched.

And as the years and the centuries passed and they did not age, they realised they were not like other people. They truly were kindred spirits.

When he hit the road, Billy felt his organs rupture, and his bones shatter. He rolled in closer towards the hedge. His skull was cracked and he was blind, though not deaf. He could hear the purr of the Jaguar's engine as it drew nearer. Then he could hear it skimming past him. He could imagine the hard-faced men sitting inside, with their guns and swords. He knew their type. He had run away from them before and always had he been caught. For they were remorseless, and there were many of them, and his kind could always be sniffed out. They had a stench that left a musky trail across the planet.

He knew Jane was a fool to think she could avoid her destiny. He wished she had not ordered him to flee with her. It was wrong of her to do that. But perhaps –

He lost consciousness and when he woke, the pain was almost unendurable. And yet, he welcomed it.

He stood up. His legs were like twigs and could barely support him. His T-shirt was ripped, the skin of his upper body hung loose on him. His tattoos were peeling from his body. His skull was fractured in – he did a quick tally – eleven places.

He started to walk, slowly, along the country road. It would take him a day to reach the city at this rate.

As he staggered onwards, his flesh began to grow back upon him.

He had lost an eyeball but he could now see well enough with the one remaining eye, and he could sense his surroundings through the flakes of ripped skin that floated above him, like a brooding thundercloud.

Billy Franco wept, through the tear gland of his surviving eye, on to a cheek that was bloodied and ripped, and the weeping hurt and made him feel alive.

Hayley was mopping blood off the floor.

That was a big part of her job, it seemed. Keeping the mortuary clean. Wiping off blood and bodily seepage. Spraying surfaces with disinfectant. She wore nose plugs some days. The sweet smell of death was with her always. It followed her home too. Even when she was in the bath, she could smell putrefaction through the scent of lavender bath oil. It was fortunate, she sometimes felt, that she was already a solitary misanthrope; otherwise this job would make her so.

The blood on the floor was not visible; there weren't huge gobbets of scarlet gore pooled upon the plastic parquet. But every time the pathologist cut open a body with an electric saw, colloids of plasma and flesh filled the air in an invisible miasma. So the floors had to be cleaned every day with immaculate care. The microscopic splashes couldn't be left to fester. The blood had to be mopped away.

Hayley wore a white coverall over her jeans and T-shirt. Her head was shaven. Every now and then she twitched her head, to reorient her lazy eye.

When Hayley was eight years old she had walked into a moving swing in the park, with bloody and painful consequences. After three days in what her Mam always called the 'hospital for stupid children', she was told she had to wear an eyepatch for six months. When the patch came off the eye had a mind of its own. She could see fine with it but it had a tendency to drift, to eerie effect.

When she was sixteen she had the huge tunnel piercings in her ears, which her Mam said made her look like a [racist expletive deleted]; and soon after that she started shaving her head. The nose piercings came next, then the tattoos, including a map of Terra Incognita on her left arm, and a more restrained blue butterfly on the soft skin under her chin.

Hayley was now twenty-six years old and no longer lived with her Mam, thank Christ; and she was wearing, beneath her mortuary-issue white coverall, on strict orders of the management, a long-sleeved top that covered the arm tattoos. The invisible blood on the floor was a bugger to get off but she was persisting.

She was thinking about songs she would sing if she could only sing. She was on stage at Glastonbury. In that context, her look was a killer. Her band was all girl and hardcore and they were playing driving chords. Hayley was singing Paranoid, and killing it. Her sister was in the crowd, crushed with jealousy. And –

She heard a sound – a groan? She ignored it. Another groan. The groan became a stifled scream.

She turned around.

The female corpse on the autopsy table was sitting up. Looking at Hayley, bold as brass. The corpse was a young woman – mid twenties or thirties, Hayley guessed. Slim, verging on skinny, with ribs you could count. Her face was smashed in and disfigured by some terrible accident. Her mouth was open in a ghastly rictus, like a silent scream. And when she spoke, her lips barely moved.

This must be a try on. Is this bitch wearing horror movie makeup?

'Help me,' the dead woman said, softly.

The dead woman had raven black hair and very pale skin and Hayley realised that she must have been beautiful, when alive, and when her face was intact. She had a soft whispery voice. The voice said: 'Please, whoever you are, help me.'

No. No! This can't be happening. Maybe I fell asleep in front of the telly again? Hayley, wake the fuck up!

'Help me, please. People are coming for me. Bad people. I have to get out of this place. Help me. I'm begging you. Help!'

Hayley tried to scream but couldn't.

'Save my baby,' whispered the corpse and Hayley flinched.

The corpse's eyes rolled, and the body slumped back down on to the stainless steel dissecting table, and was once more inert.

And now, finally, Hayley screamed.

Billy Franco, once known as Will Darke, and before that William Prentis, was standing outside the Leeds Hospital Mortuary and every atom of his being told him that his one true love was inside this building. And he yearned to have the courage to go in and rescue her.

He thought of all the times over the years when she had cherished him, and protected him. He remembered the days of Queen Mary, when he had been burned at the stake, and she had carefully carried his embers away and watered them daily until his lips were moist again. He remembered the time he lost his mind and she had to lock him in a room for almost a year before his gibbering stopped. He remembered the hundred years he had spent as an Andromeda; and the moment when he had emerged from the castle in Scotland, wasted and skeletal and pale, and drained of all but a cup of his own blood, and she had been waiting for him patiently in her car. Her love undimmed.

Philip Palmer

He owed her everything. She was so brave. So fearless.

Not like him. He was a coward even before the powers that be had captured him, and worked on his mind, to drill him in obedience. That was – when? Yes, he did recall – it was early in the reign of the first King Charles. That bloody dandy. Then there was the civil war, he and Ursula missed most of that. They were locked in that house in Kent being taught about theology and Divine Retribution, and learning that they were God's children after all, even though they reeked of sin.

He remembered the many years they lived apart, forced to live with human masters, learning obedience and reverence to God. And yet somehow, at the end of his hundred years in the Scottish castle chained to a wall, she had managed to track him down. And they were reunited.

And so they fled. And they had lived as man and wife, without human masters, in a myriad different identities, from 1929 until 1948. Until, once more, some immortal traitor-to-their-kind had caught their scent. And they were tagged, and monitored, but otherwise left free to live their lives in a small house in Liverpool.

Then came the day, less than three months ago, when Jane was told she had been chosen. She had been instructed that it was now time for her to do her duty, to become an Andromeda. And she had raged, and ranted, and refused And then – then they had fled, once again.

It took the Defenders a scant eleven weeks to find them.

She's in there, Billy thought. *Still alive, I'm sure of that. A crash wouldn't kill her. She probably crashed the car deliberately, knowing that would cause a fuss, and make it harder for them to take her. So I should – why don't I –*

No. If I try to save her, I'll be spotted, he thought. *They'll have spies everywhere. On the alert for one such as me. Ready to capture me and use me abominably in her place. Could I bear that again? Could I endure another hundred years of – of –*

But I have to save her! She is my beloved. If I do not I am shamed!

Yet courage eluded him. He did not dare go into the mortuary. Besides, if he did, he reasoned, what could he actually do? Carry out her broken corpse in his arms? It was absurd. He could see at a glance how hard it would be to smuggle her from this place of humans. Security guards were everywhere.

She should have accepted her fate, he told himself. *Why did she not? After all, I did, when it was my turn. What crazy folly made her act the way she –*

He remembered her resolve. Her determination. She had a plan, she said. She had fake ID, she had a car, she had money. She was confident she knew a way to elude the spies who followed them on a daily basis. Come with me, she had said. We'll live together in freedom, she had said. We'll make a new life for ourselves, she had said. We'll be just like we were in the old days. And he had followed her. Well of course he had followed her. It was in his nature to follow. They had trained him to follow. And to obey.

Defeat wrapped itself around Billy's heart. He remembered how glorious they had once been, he and she, as runaways arriving in London back in the days of Henry Tudor. He remembered the crowds and the stench of the Thames and the bustling energy of the streets.

Billy knew himself to be unworthy of her, his one true love. Despite all their 'training', their indoctrination, she remained herself. A burning flame of herness. She was so courageous!

But he was not. He never had been, in truth. Sheer terror had taken him out of that plague pit.

Billy was conscious that too much time had already passed. Within twelve hours or less from the moment of her 'death', her blood would sour and her immortality would be gone. She would become dead meat. He knew this, but did nothing about it.

Instead, he found a pub and tried to get drunk. That, too, proved impossible. After fifteen pints he was barred by an angry and bewildered landlord, but he was still icily sober.

Forgive me, Ursula.

'Sorry to keep you waiting,' said the younger copper with the blond hair and the steely blue eyes.

Hayley knew damn well that he wasn't sorry. Not one bit. He was one of those whippet-lean types, with a gaze like a headmaster crushing the will of a first former who has dared to jog down the corridor.

She kept her good eye focused on the centre of the younger copper's face, and hoped the bad eye didn't drift.

'Just a few questions, lass,' said the older copper, in bluff, friendly tones. He was heavily set, with a huge beer belly and an unruly head of black hair, and a trustworthy look. His accent was local. He was smiling at her encouragingly, in a father-figure kind of a way. Hayley took against him instantly.

'Do we have to do this?' she sneered. 'I made a mistake, right, end of story.'

'Let's just take a few details, madam, if you don't mind,' the younger copper said, briskly. His accent was also Yorkshire, but he sounded posh to her. 'I'm DS Smith, this is DC Barraclough.' The younger one out-ranked the older one, she noted; bet *that* stung. 'Can you confirm your name and age and occupation?'

'Hayley. Hayley Faith Bradley, twenty-six. I'm a makework temporary contract might as well be bloody slave labour gofer.'

'That's not an actual job title.'

'I'm assistant to the mortuary technician.'

'How long have you worked in the mortuary?'

She shrugged, thought back. 'Six months.'

'And can you tell us about the events that took place on your shift? Just start at the beginning, take us through it.'

Hayley, you daft bitch – don't forget to lie.

'Nothing to say, like. Reflex cadaveric spasm. Gases in the gut. I freaked out. Ran to the office, told the boss. He told me it was – he laughed his bollocks off, to be honest – told me it was reflex cadaveric spasms, caused by gases in the gut. I felt so daft. Sorry, sorry.' She was blinking now, that old habit was back. 'Sorry.'

'Just tell us what you saw.'

'I saw – the body –'

Oh fucking hell.

She remembered: The body sitting up. Still wearing its bloody clothes from the crash, the face bloodied and scarred, the throat jaggedly cut, the eyes staring, saying: 'Please, whoever you are, help me!'

'I ah.' Hayley took a breath. She couldn't risk coming across as a crazy woman. 'The post mortem was due to be performed at 4pm. My job was to strip the body and prepare the instruments. Then it –'

Hayley remembered: The dead woman's hand reaching out, fumbling for contact, her fingers splayed...

'Then,' Hayley said, 'the body seemed to twitch and I thought I heard a groan and I panicked. So I went to see my boss and he laughed, I told you all about that.'

'That's your immediate boss, Larry Braxton. '

'That's right.'

'Chief mortuary technician.'

'He's the only mortuary technician, I'm just the assistant.'

'There's no chance the body could have been, like, alive?' said the older one, with an attempt at a genial twinkle.

Hayley made a 'duh' face.

But in fact, that's what she had thought at first. That they'd fucked it up at A&E. And she'd said so to Larry and to the pathologist, and to one of the doctors who had come down for something.

And then everyone had started bullshitting her, using that annoying grown-up tone. Saying Oh no! A thing like that could never happen here, not in *our* hospital.

You silly girl, Hayley.

Ah, another trip to the hospital for stupid children.

You are such a retard!

Mam, shut up! Don't tell me –

Hayley knew a cover up when she saw one. That's why she'd called the cops.

But in the twenty minutes before the cops arrived, the pathologist had explained the medical reality to Hayley, with painstaking care.

'Now listen carefully, Hayley.' Sweet smile.

Oh God. This again.

The body, Hayley was told at length, had been partially decapitated after hitting the windscreen at speed. An artery in the victim's neck had been severed and blood loss was very severe. After being pronounced dead at A&E the body had lain lifeless on a hospital trolley for more than four hours. Rigor mortis had subsequently set in.

Mistakes happen, but no one ever recovers from that kind of dead, the pathologist gently explained. And so Hayley – bless her – was making a fool of herself.

'Watching too many scary movies, perhaps' was the phrase that stung the most.

'Answer the question please,' said the older copper. 'Could the body have been alive?'

'No,' said Hayley. 'Course not, mate. The PM has been rescheduled, it goes ahead tomorrow morning. End of story, like.'

The younger one shrugged. False alarm, waste of time.

'Thank you for your assistance.'

'No probs.'

Hayley stood up.

The younger one was staring oddly at her. She guessed it was her hair. It was purple today, with lime green highlights: a ghastly combination.

Pissed off at this attention, she licked her lips, to give him a better look at her tongue stud. That freaked out most blokes, though a few loved it.

But she knew it was the eye. No matter what she did to her appearance, blokes homed in on the drifting dead eye. It was not, hand on heart, her best feature.

'Take care of yourself, love,' the older one said. DC Barraclough was his name, she recalled. He was looking at her too, but not unkindly.

'Are we done?'

'We're done,' Barraclough said firmly.

'Right then,' she said, and she turned and with a few brisk strides was gone. Out of their fucking hair.

In the corridor she stopped and took a breath.

And she remembered the lips that didn't move, pleading with her:

'Save my baby.'

'Sweetheart, please don't do that ever again,' Larry said to Hayley, half an hour later.

Larry was a broad man; that's the first thing you noticed about him. Short, stocky, bald, tanned, with strong beefy arms.

'I won't – I didn't mean to – I'm sorry, Larry.'

'You made us all look like prats.' His words were harsh, but as always his tone was gentle.

'Just panicked. Sorry.'

Larry nodded, eventually.

'Have they gone now?'

'No. They want to view the body.'

Hayley was startled. 'Why?'

Larry made a face: how the fuck should I know?

'You're so good to me, Larry,' Hayley babbled.

He grinned, shyly. 'Someone has to look after you, right?'

'I appreciate it.'

'No need. Only too happy.' He was red with embarrassment now. Good old Larry. Where would she be without him?

There was a knock at the office door. The older cop, Barraclough, opened the door, wanting attention. Larry got up and joined him, without a backwards glance.

Hayley was left behind. She dithered. Her curiosity was killing her, like a toothache.

I'll be quick about it.

She moved around and sat in Larry's chair. She dabbed a key to unsleep the computer. Typed a user name: LBRAXTON59. Typed a password: MICKEY98. Larry's dog, and the dog's birth year. Then she typed a patient name.

CARTER, JANE ALLISON.

A PDF file appeared; she opened it. She scrolled down the file. Body brought in to Wetherby A & E Wednesday 25th of June at 10.30am, after failed attempts at resuscitation by paramedics in the ambulance. Brain damage was considered to be irreversible. The death was called at 10.45am. The body was then taken to the seventh floor. Following the new protocols, a CT scan was performed, and also an MRI and then – Hayley felt a surge of interest.

The body had already been autopsied, electronically.

Hayley carried on looking. A 3D computer-modelled image of the body flicked on to the screen. It was a remarkable portrait of the entirety of a human being, like Leonardo's Vitruvian Man. Except you could see the inside of the body as well as the outside. Hayley knew how to read it; she zoomed and toggled.

Larry trudged with the coppers into the cadaver room. Part of him was enjoying this. Any disruption to the daily grind was worth something.

'I do have a job to do, you know,' Larry grumbled, out of habit.

'Just routine, sir,' DS Smith said, in the same tone another man might use to say fuck off and die.

'Yeah yeah.'

'Thank you for your assistance, sir,' Barraclough chipped in.

'Whatever.'

Larry walked them to the cold chamber. He yanked the drawer open. The body of CARTER, JANE ALLISON rolled out on its metal tray, and slid on to the trolley in a single smooth movement. Larry pushed the switches and the crossed arms of the hydraulic trolley lowered. The corpse descended to hip level.

'Help yourself.'

The older copper, Barraclough, zippered open the white body bag, revealing the face of the RTA victim. Larry glimpsed blood and gristle and looked away.

'You should wear gloves.'

'I'll be fine,' Barraclough said, tersely.

Barraclough pulled the zipper down further, exposing the bloody mess of the torso.

'She wanted for something?'

'We're pursuing lines of investigation,' said DS Smith, with a thin, false smile.

Larry gave them an 'abashed' look. 'Sorry about that, earlier, with the girl like. We take what we get, you see. Last year we had an albino boy, he hardly spoke. Like a bloody ghost.' Larry shook his head, bemoaning the incompetence of his staff past, present and future.

Barraclough opened up his shoulder bag, took out a live-scan machine. No bigger than a credit card reader. Calmly, with practised ease, Barraclough fingerprinted the corpse's right hand using the scanner. He was methodical. In the old days he'd have used an ink roller for this process and gone home with black marks on his fingers.

'Who identified the body?' Smith asked.

'No one yet.'

'No one?'

'There's a husband, apparently. Someone left a message. That's all I know. '

Smith looked at Barraclough.

Barraclough took a deep breath through his nose; exhaled through his mouth. Then again. Then he nodded. Smith acknowledged with the faintest of facial movements.

Larry saw all this but thought nothing of it.

He didn't realise that these two had been tracking and controlling this woman for more than twenty years. He didn't know she'd been tagged, and told where to live, and who to live with, since just after World War II. He had no idea that in 21st century Britain such a state of abject slavery could still exist, or be state-sanctioned. He just thought the two coppers were making a mountain out of a, well, a nothing very much at all.

Hayley kept reviewing the findings. Maybe there was a mistake. A smudge on the screen? She wiped the computer screen with her thumb. No smudge.

Christ on a bloody stick. What am I going to do?

Answer: Nothing. Pretend this never happened. Pretend you didn't see –

No, fuck that.

Let's think about this logically. Problem: No one can know I'm accessing these files. Or I'll be in the shit. However, I can't keep what I've found out a secret. It's too big a thing. Front page story stuff.

So maybe I could make an anonymous call? But who do I call? And what can I possibly say that doesn't make me sound like a bloody nutter?

On the screen, in full magnification, was the MRI image of the brain of

Carter, Jane Allison. It had a shadow inside. An object the size of a small egg. A tumour? Or a bomb? Hayley had seen the episode of Spooks in which –

She heard a sound at the door. The computer was put to sleep in an instant. Hayley took a handful of forms from the in tray and pretended to read them. Larry appeared at the door; peeking his head around the frame, but not his body. An oddly comic effect.

'You still here?'

'Evidently.'

'You can knock off. Try and behave tomorrow, okay?'

'Yes, Larry. Thanks.'

Larry sighed, with exaggerated indulgence, and withdrew his head.

Wanker, Hayley thought. And immediately felt guilty. He might be fat and bald and gross but Larry had always been lovely to her. Really kind. She ought to be more grateful.

Hayley at ten years of age. Brown hair that didn't sit up right and didn't take product. Freckles like cancer patches. The eyepatch. The attitude. Sent home from school yet again, this time for calling her teacher a 'cunt'.

'Do you even know what that is, you stupid, offensive, waste-of-space little brat?' her Mam had asked her. Mam was half pissed, of course, it was nearly half past four by this point.

'It's what you are. Mam the cunt!'

If you expect and anticipate a punch to the face, Hayley always found, it actually hurts just as much. Was that one of life's lessons, maybe?

'How can I help you guys?' Detective Inspector Taylor asked, warily.

Barraclough said nothing. He just offered up his warrant card. Smith did the litany: 'I'm DS Smith, this is DC Barraclough. We're from Wetherby nick.'

When he was a young man, Harry Barraclough used to help the village constable light the gas lamps. There were two, one outside the farrier's and the other outside the pub. That was a job that was – lighting the lamps!

Now, he worked for Leeds CID and he carried a mobile phone and used the internet on a daily basis. That's how it goes. Time passes; things change. Harry remembered the old days fondly, but that was an eternity ago now, or so it seemed.

It was all very different now. Ever since the day, back in 1956 it was, when there was a knock on the door of his cottage, and when he opened it, instead of seeing the Queen standing there clutching a telegram with a big smile on her face, as he was fondly and daftly expecting, he saw two men with those weird electricity-guns who pulsed him to the ground and took him into custody. Anxious, they later explained, to find out why an ordinary bloke like him bore no visible signs of ageing.

Harry tried, he really did, not to be bitter about how much his life had changed since the powers that be discovered he was immortal.

'Pleased to meet you. I'm DI Taylor.'

'Yeah we know that.'

Taylor shrugged. He shook hands with each of them in turn. Smith and Barraclough took the seats on offer.

Harry took the measure of the other copper with a swift glance. Smooth, silver-haired. Easygoing, verging on lazy, was Harry's guess.

'We're looking into an RTA that happened yesterday morning, sir. Jean Carter, sir.' Smith said, brusquely.

Smith was the youngest man in the room, and junior in rank to Taylor. But he carried with him an air of effortless authority. And when he said 'sir', he might as well have said 'fuck you'. Harry was used to it; most folk weren't.

Taylor picked up a file – the only file on his desk. He riffled through it.

'Jean Allison Carter,' he said, reading from his notes. 'Hit by a lorry. Head on collision. There's a depot, you see, just outside Leeds, the lorry was heading for the main road. She took the corner at speed, it wasn't his fault. Front of the car was totally caved in. Her air bag didn't work. It was an old car, she'd never had it checked.'

'Why?' Smith's manner was abrupt, as if he spent his life talking to idiots and was getting fed up of it.

'Why what?' Taylor said patiently.

'Why did she take the corner at speed?'

'Bad driving?'

'Was there a vehicle in pursuit?'

Taylor stared. 'Not that I know of.'

'Skid marks?'

Taylor checked his notes again. 'We did a skid mark analysis to determine the speed of the respective vehicles. You're welcome to read the report from the Collisions Investigation Unit. A reconstruction was performed, we estimate that Carter was driving at eighty-five, maybe ninety miles an hour on a winding country road. The lorry was doing forty-nine, below the legal limit for the road. Carter was –'

'Yes but where was she going? And from where?'

'She lived in Harrogate, she was on the road to Leeds.'

'We need to inspect the scene.'

'You're better off looking at the photos and the laser scans.'

'We need to inspect the scene.'

Barraclough nodded in a friendly fashion to Taylor. His manner silently disowned Smith's flat, annoyed tone.

Taylor nodded back at Barraclough. No sweat, I'm used to this; that was his nod. His tone remained friendly. 'I'll get one of my men to drive you out there. What's the context?'

'Ongoing investigation.'

Taylor shrugged, not taking offence. 'Lorry driver not to blame, as I say. He's in shock, really. '

'We'll need his name and address, as well as the details of his place of work. Sir.'

'No worries.' Taylor leaned back, relaxed, inviting confidences. 'What was she up to then, our lady driver?'

Smith smiled thinly. Said nothing.

Barraclough favoured Taylor with a smile. 'She's red flagged as part of a major CID case, sir. We were hoping to interview her.'

'Too late now.'

'Aye, that's true enough.'

The two men shared a moment.

Smith glared at Taylor; all business.

'I'll get you those details now,' Taylor said. 'Just wait here.'

'You got to wear the horns. You got to!'

Let me die now, Hayley thought sadly.

All she had wanted to do was crawl into bed and forgot everything that had happened in the course of this terrible day. Instead, she was stuck making nice with her sister Cheyney. Her younger sister Cheyney. Who, to Hayley's horror, was now clad in the full fishnet stockings, clingy basque and pushed-up cleavage cliché. She looked like wassername from Cabaret. Sally Bowles. But with more flesh on her bones, admittedly. And in fairness, the devil horns looked great on her. They were bright scarlet. Wrapped around with black fur. Cheyney danced to an imaginary Rihanna song and jiggled her head and twerked and the horns tottered on her head.

Hayley stared at her baby sister with a despair honed by years of practice. She'd come home early for *this?* She felt like a cow having its throat cut in the abattoir.

'I mean – Jesus, Chey – this is not my – I don't go for this kind of –' she said, and ran out of words.

'You don't like to be sexy?' Cheyney taunted her.

Nasty. Hayley *never* looked sexy. That was her 'thing'.

'This is not sexy, it's slutty.'

Cheyney rolled her eyes. 'That's the, like, point?'

'You look like a whore!'

'The word is 'ho'!'

'That's what I said!'

'You so did not,' Cheyney mocked her, as if her magic ears could tell the difference.

Hen Parties. They actually call them Hen Parties! Cluck cluck cluck!

'Why do women want to dress like whores? 'Ho's? Whores!' Hayley said, with the same degree of stunned bafflement she had applied to algebra and computational analysis, back in Barton Street Comp.

'Cause it's funny?'

'Sexist!'

'Can't be sexist, cause I'm a woman!'

'Can be, too, you're just pandering to the –'

'Don't say patriarchy. I mean, for fuck's sake, it's Twenty Nineteen, no one says 'patriarchy'!'

That's so not fair, I wasn't – okay, well maybe I was going to say 'patriarchy'. Is that so terrible?

'I didn't say –'

'Well don't.'

'But if I did –'

'Just don't. Or you'll never get –'

'I'll wear the horns. Not the rest.'

'It'll be a right laugh.'

'It'll be a stupid embarrassing piss up from Hell and I'll end up puking in the front garden, again.'

'Don't be so sad, chuck.'

'I'm not sad. I'm not your fucking chuck.'

'We'll still –'You're my sister. Get married. See if I care.'

Cheyney grinned. Irrepressible. She pranced around the bedroom to some fresh Rihanna moves. It was ridiculous! Though she did have the look for it, in fairness; the sisters had the same black dad but Cheyney's skin was a glorious rock star coffee colour, while Hayley was so pale she might as well be white.

'We're good?'

'Yeah yeah.'

'And you're happy for me?'

'Course.'

'And you love Liam almost as much as I do?'

No I fucking don't! He's a lying thieving womanising piece of –

'Yes, of course I do.'

'I love you, bro.'

'Not your bro!'

'Sis, then.'

'Not cis, that means the opposite of –'

'Whatever.' Cheyney grinned.

Oh Cheyney, how do you do it? How do you manage to be so bloody happy all the time?

Cheyney was full-bodied and beautiful. Her smile could cut the hardest heart at a thousand paces. Hayley felt tired and sexless just looking at her.

'I just want you to, you know, enjoy yourself.'

'Whatever.'

'You need to join in a bit more.'

The words hurt Hayley, like knives in the heart.

'I will. I said I will.' Hayley became aware that she was stony-faced, and her voice had a shriek of desperation. 'I will. I fucking will, all right!'

Join in. Why should I want to join in? What's so great about –

Oh fuck it.

'Yeah. Great.' Cheyney blew her sister a kiss; but Hayley didn't catch it, or blow one back, like a proper girl would have done.

'Where's the stag night going to be?' Hayley asked, grudgingly.

'Oh he's not having one. You think I'd fucking trust *him?*'

'DS Smith, DC Barraclough.'

The bald-headed weird-looking man stared at them. 'Yeah?'

'Are you Tony Riley?'

'I am.'

'We want to talk about the accident you had yesterday.'

'Do you now? Ah. Right. Well. I guess so. Come on, sit down. Are you

Smith?'

'I'm Barraclough.'

'I'm Jack. You must be Smith then?'

'That's correct, sir.'

They all sat down. They were in the staff canteen of the tobacco warehouse outside Leeds where the lorry driver worked. It was just after 7pm. He was Tony Riley, thirty-four, born in Doncaster. Back at work despite being involved in a fatal accident less than twenty-four hours ago.

Riley was young, shaven headed, Hebrew phrases tattooed on his neck. He had a twitchy intensity. And an obsession with avoiding eye contact that screamed 'paedo pervert', though in fact he was not.

Out of habit, Barraclough sniffed him. Out of habit, Smith shot him a look. Barraclough shook his head, so faintly you had to be a student of micro-gestures to recognise it as a shaking of the head. But Smith was expert at reading his chattel's signs. He visibly relaxed.

The canteen was half-full, over-lit, furnished with garish red plastic chairs, plastic tables and colour-coded recycling bins.

'You know that the other driver died in hospital.'

Twitch; stare; rueful look. 'Yeah they told me that.'

'We just want to ask some questions.'

'Weren't my fault. Weren't.'

'We're not saying it was, Tony.' Barraclough gave him his full bluff Yorkshiremen-together smile. 'She was driving too fast, it's cut and dried.'

'You're not going to arrest me for manslaughter then?'

'Hell no, Tony. She came round the corner like a bat out of hell, didn't she?'

'She did that.'

'That was your phrase, wasn't it?'

'Might have been. I was coming from here, see. Out of the depot. We have three miles to drive on a country road before we hit the main drag. Not much traffic though. But I turned the bend, a blind bend, and there she was. Coming right at me like –'

'Did you see another vehicle?' Smith said abruptly.

'What?'

'Did you see another vehicle behind her. In pursuit?'

'No. Was she being –?'

'Just answer the question.'

'No.'

'So what happened? After you saw her?'

'I braked, and thought about swerving, but I didn't have time. So I hit her, like. Front on collision. I ended up in the hedge, lorry slewed right along the road, and when I got out, her car was, well, it had crumpled.'

'And then what?'

'And then I called the ambulance.'

'No, back up. One moment at a time. Your lorry crashed. Then what?'

'Airbag inflated. I deflated it. Got out of the cab. Got me bearings back. Then I looked around, saw her car. Then I called the ambulance. What else can I say?'

'You can say what you saw.'

'Nothing. Car was crashed. She was –'

'She was what?'

'Alive. She was alive. I pulled the door open. Pulled her out. She was alive. Blood was gushing out of her throat, and she was puking up blood too, big gobbets of it. Blood was everywhere. I tried to put her in the recovery position, but I couldn't –'

'You have first aid training?'

'Aye I do. But I've never seen anything like this. She was –'

'Head on collision. Severed artery in the neck. Internal bleeding. She was still alive when you reached the car. That's pretty straightforward,' Smith said coldly.

'Must have been traumatic,' said Barraclough, soothing.

'You're not listening to me. I've never – she puked blood. On the road. And she looked at me. And the blood –'

'What?'

'I can't say it.'

'Say it.'

'The blood was on the ground. But it started to, like,' He whispered the word: 'move.'

'Move?

'Boil. Her blood was boiling, like a mist, like.'

'That's not possible, blood cannot boil at normal atmospheric –'

'It fucking did, aye? A mist of blood, dancing like bloody – whatever – in front of her body, then she opened her mouth and the blood flew up into the air and she drank it in. Drank her own blood.'

'Now that didn't really happen, did it?' said Barraclough gently.

'I'm saying what I saw. It was blood like – like it had a life of its own. Like – gnats – you know, in Scotland you get the midges. Hovering in the air like –'

'She inhaled some of her own blood, that can happen.'

The driver shook his head, stubborn. 'I've googled it, it's happened before. It's a recognised 'strange' phenomenon. It's –'

'You're talking Fortean Times bullshit, sir, you're talking what is basically nonsense.' Smith's tone was scornful, unprofessionally so.

'It's not nonsense. In Mexico, a woman was stabbed. And the blood came out of her body and formed a halo in the air. A halo! And it stayed there, for minutes, until she died. Two old women saw it, the paramedics too. It was a miracle, the Catholics said. There's one thread that argues –'

'I think, sir, you need counselling, it's been a very traumatic time for you .'

'I know what I saw.'

'You're stressed, sir.'

'Happen I am. Even so –'

'We're done here,' said Smith, abruptly.

He stood up. Barraclough reluctantly stood too.

That night, Barraclough wrote up his notes in the old school exercise books he had purchased from a Ragged School in Lancashire. In his immaculate copperplate handwriting he wrote a detailed diary of everyone he had met that day and everything they had said.

His notes included an account of the mobile phone conversation Smith had in the lorry park of the tobacco warehouse, after their interview with Tony Riley. Barraclough had been banished out of earshot, of course, but he took the precaution of spitting on his finger and wiping it on one of the lorries.

While Barraclough paced around the lorry park, his saliva had listened intently to Smith's side of the phone call with the powers that be. Smith had sounded agitated. He was clearly under criticism for allowing CARTER, JANE ALLISON to escape from the high speed pursuit. Now that she was in a public mortuary, it would be much harder to retrieve her body. But retrieve it they would – though Barraclough had no idea why.

There was some internal politics going on, too, among the various factions of the Powers that Be, Bararclough had gleaned that from some of Smith's sardonic mutterings. He wrote all that down too.

Drummond – who is he and why does no one like him?

The old chief, mentioned twice now. That must be

Rothbury, Marlowe used to know him. Cruel man. One of the worst I have known. Not seen him in a good while, I wonder why.

A large nest in Bradford. Near the Midland Hotel. That's news to me.

Smith said 'Yes sir' twice in that emphatic tone of his, and I'm guessing he has been given his Actions. My guess also is that they are loose end Actions. Retreival First. Then Tony Riley is TWP. And after that or concurrently, Hayley Bradly will also be Terminated.

Shame, I liked her.

Hayley was suffering. Sandpaper mouth. Stomach howling for sausage roll, or cold pasty, or something, anything, to fill the void. Head pounding. The god of temperance was banging her skull rebukingly upon a hard marble floor.

'Right, love? Christ, you look like death warmed up.'

Larry was smiling at her. She'd warned him not to smile so much when she had a hangover but there was no restraining some people.

'Hen night go okay, did it?'

'What do you think?' Her tone was insolent. But Larry let it slide.

'I expect it was great,' he said, cheerfully. 'I bet everyone had a fabulous time. After all, women dressed like sluts, cheap supermarket booze, what could go wrong?'

'Uh.'

'You did talk to people, didn't you?'

'Uh.'

'Did you?'

'A bit.' But her body language said no.

'Oh Hayley.' Larry was still smiling. His bald head was shining. His cheeks were rosy. Even the deep furrows in his brow seemed smiley.

Hayley knew that Larry was up at six every morning in the park, walking the dog, before coming to work. The best part of the day, he always called it.

It was now ten am.

'You're late,' he said gently.

'I'll mop the floor. I'm *not* opening up any bodies today,' she warned him. 'Or putting any organs in, yuk.'

'You can mop the floor.'

She shrugged, grudging.

There is one thing,' he added lightly.

'Yeah? Wazzat?'

'That woman. The cadaveric spasm woman.'

Hayley shrugged. 'Made a fool of,' she mumbled, not finishing her sentence; that always drove Larry mad. But today he kept smiling.

'Maybe it wasn't,' he said, cheerily.

Huh?'

'Maybe she, you know.' He winked.

He was winding her up, she realised.

Oh boy.

'Sorry, okay? Sorry, sorry —'

'Oh, I had a call from the seventh floor.' Larry's tone was still casual.

'Yeah?'

'The seventh floor,' he prompted.

'I know where the seventh floor is. It's on the, ah.' She let it go.

'Apparently they had a security alert yesterday.'

'Well, nothing to do with me. I was down here.'

'A computer security alert. Someone accessing medical files without authorisation, and without a credible reason.'

'You're kidding me?'

'They think it was me.'

'Yeah?'

'Yeah.'

Oh shit. Who would have thought they'd have noticed?

'It wasn't me, though,' Larry explained.

'No.'

'It was someone —'

'I get it — I get it — it was me. No harm done.'

Lighten up for fuck's sake, Larry, it's not like I was checking out your porn collection.

'What were you playing at, Hayley?'

'I just wanted to – I was curious.'

'You looked at the virtopsy for Jane Carter.'

She wriggled. 'I was curious.'

'Why, Hayley?' The kind tone still: that was the killer.

'It just seemed odd.' Hayley glared at him. She saw him flinch from her dead eye gaze. 'You see, it wasn't really a –'

'What?'

'Spasm.'

'No?'

'She spoke.'

'Dead women tell no tales,' joshed Larry.

'I didn't imagine it.'

'Of course you imagined it.'

Hayley made a face.

'The virtopsy,' Larry chided.

'Yeah, well, I thought,' said Hayley. 'When I saw she'd had one, I thought – take a look, why not?'

The virtopsy – the virtual autopsy – was a state of the art technique being trialled at Wetherby General. The technique offered a way of ascertaining cause of death without the need to open up the corpse. Larry hated it on principle: his life's work was opening up corpses.

'And what did it reveal?'

The findings had seemed, to Hayley, to be bizarre. The dead woman's heart was abnormally large, half again as large as one would expect from a woman of that size. The alveoli in the lungs were over-developed. The musculature was astonishingly dense. These were results you might from a marathon runner who was also an Olympic gymnast. But the dead woman, so the notes said, was an office worker from Harrogate.

'She kept herself fit.'

'You're not allowed,' said Larry kindly, 'to access medical data. It's a sacking offence, you know. And on top of what you did earlier yesterday, calling the police in for no reason, well, you could be for the high jump. Considering you're only temporary in the first place. And considering, too, that a lot of people don't see things as – generously – as I do. They don't have my – deep-seated interest in your wellbeing, hmm? Do you grasp that, flower, do you follow what I'm saying?'

He twinkled. And waited. He let the silence do his work for him. Hayley's bafflement started to fade, to be replaced by anxious dread.

Larry was still waiting for her to concede that she grasped what he was saying. She finally nodded.

'I didn't mean any harm.' Her little girl voice; she hated it.

I'm such a fucking fool.

'I could get you in serious trouble,' said Larry. 'Or I could, alternatively, get you out of serious trouble. Those are the two options really.' She was acutely aware that Larry was totally bald, apart from those wisps of grey in front of his stubby ears. And aware too, vividly aware, of his wrinkles, the thick set ridges in his rhino flesh. And aware also that he was old, fifty at least. Hayley steeled herself.

'I'm so sorry, please don't get me into trouble, Larry, hmm?' There it was again: a scared little girl someone burst my balloon voice.

If he touches me I'll kick him in the fucking balls.

'Well I'll try my best. I like you, Hayley.' Larry got up. He seemed unnaturally short because his body was so wide, but even so he towered over her. 'But this is an official warning. Don't access medical files. Don't snoop. You're just an assistant to the assistant, never forget that.'

Stern face yielded to forgiving smiley face. He reached out: offering a hug.

Hayley stood up and stepped forward. She stood rigidly and let him hug her. His arms patted her back consolingly, even though she wasn't weeping, nowhere near it. No inappropriate touching took place however. No hand on the arse.

Maybe he's just being nice?

'Good girl, Hayley,' he whispered, his head close to hers, and his lips brushed her hair.

Oh Jesus.

Larry let go. Stepped back. Still smiling. 'Mop, dissection room, I think you know the drill.'

'Yeah sure, Larry.'

He was looking her up and down. What did he want?

'You might say thank you,' Larry said, aggrieved.

'Sorry. Thank you, Larry.'

'You're welcome.'

Later that day, at the end of the afternoon, Hayley read the pathologist's post mortem report on *Carter, Jane Allison* with astonishment. Same findings: larger organs than might be expected for a woman of this size, highly developed musculature. Cause of death cerebral haemorrhage, consistent with the massive trauma of being hit by a lorry at speed and hurled through a car windscreen, combined with blood loss due to the severing of the carotid artery. Damage to internal organs, three broken ribs, bleeding into the lungs. Arms and legs broken in several places.

But the physical sectioning and analysis of the brain had revealed no foreign objects. No egg-like thing. And yet the MRI image was crystal clear. No room for doubt. So what was going on?

Would the pathologist have seen the virtopsy? Hayley wondered. Did he know what to look for? And could he just have missed it, the egg-like thing?

But he couldn't have missed it! That was impossible! Unless – unless – A resolve formed in Hayley's mind.

Too many scary movies?

I'll fucking show 'em.

Hayley went home at 6pm then walked back to the hospital again at 10pm. The mortuary was locked up but Hayley had keys, she didn't have to break in. She had no legal basis for re-entering her place of work, however. And even when she was on duty she wasn't allowed to touch the bodies except to strip them. She felt weird; she'd never done anything like this before. But it was exciting. Telly-thrillerish, really.

The dissecting room had fluorescent lights dating from the 1970s that leeched the sheen from the stainless steel of the autopsy tables and the sinks. She blinked, gagging on the stench of the vicious detergent the cleaners laid down each night.

Hayley blinked again. The overhead lights always irked her good eye; they gave her migraines sometimes. She was wearing jeans and a hoodie but she took the hoodie off and underneath she had an old T-shirt she'd once used to paint the hall. Smeared and filthy and not washed since she'd stuck it in the wardrobe.

She put on latex gloves and disposable overalls and with a flourish, donned a face mask and goggles. Then she strode into the next room where the cold chambers were housed, and identified the correct door from the hand drawn map sellotaped to the wall. She opened the top right chamber where CARTER, JANE ALLISON was being stored. Once a junior manager with an insurance firm. Now, naked and ice-cold on the silvery body tray. Her pale flesh marked with scars from the crash and the pathologist's probing knife.

Hayley used the hydraulic trolley to transfer the body out of the chamber. She wheeled it back into the dissecting room. She was trembling now from proximity to the freezer-chilled air, and from fear. She could be sacked for what she was about to do. She could go to jail.

Why am I doing this?

The answer was obvious. Her pulse was racing, her hearing was unnaturally acute, she could smell every rank trace of the body and the chemicals in the dissecting room, and she was even able to feel the crackle of the air from the fluorescent lights. She'd never been good at sports but she knew this must be what it felt like to run the hundred metres at a record speed, or score the winning goal. Adrenalin high; endorphin rush: it was the thing she'd heard so much about but never experienced. It was the buzz.

Okay, so danger turns me on. I never knew that.

She zippered open the body bag to expose the head. Same woman; same raven-black hair; definitely dead. Like a waxwork dummy, not sinister, just unreal. The fissure on the skull was visible, running from ear to ear; this was where the pathologist had opened up the cranium to remove the brain in order to dissect it.

Hayley picked up a scalpel and hacked at the old cuts, chiselling away clumsily, tugging at the bone as if she were levering up an old floorboard.

Then, latex gloves slick with blood, she rocked the skullcap until it came away. She removed the dura mater, a scary little thing, and put it on the sink. The brain was now exposed, as pinkly raw as a wrinkled peach. Hayley blinked. She was sweating but didn't want to wipe her brow.

She lifted the brain out of the cranium, carefully; it was in parts, in a plastic bag. She placed it on the metal sink that was a built-in part of the autopsy table. Now she wiped her brow, with a bare forearm.

She remembered to breathe: and did so, swiftly.

She took Jane Carter's brain out of its plastic covering. It had been sectioned with a brain knife, then put back together like pieces of a jigsaw. She eased the pieces apart until it resembled a loaf sliced by a greedy child.

She tried to remember the placing of the foreign object in the MRI. Middle of the brain? She inspected each section in turn. Then she took off the goggles and looked each part of the cerebrum through binocular loupes. Still no trace of any foreign object. Finally, exasperated, she picked up each slice of brain in turn and fumbled inside the cerebral matter with her fingers, like a toddler searching for the threepenny bit in a Christmas pudding. And on the third go she felt a lump. She pulled it out.

An object, hidden inside the victim's brain.

Oh boy.

She could visualise the headlines: LEEDS WOMAN FOILS TERROR

PLOT.

It occurred to her that if this were indeed a bomb, it might blow up. Time, perhaps, to exit at haste, and call the cops.

But she had to find out more. She peered at the object. It was like a very small egg. Exactly the same diameter as the brain slices she had cut. That in itself was bizarre. She dabbed at the object with a latexed fingertip. Soft to the touch. Not metal, then. Not a bomb, then. So was it just a tumour? Had this woman been carrying an undiagnosed tumour the size of a pigeon's egg?

She looked closer. She lifted the scalpel and went to cut into the surface –

The egg-like thing moved.

She put the scalpel down. The egg-like thing was still. She picked it up again. The egg-like thing moved, slithering away from her on the metal table.

This must be how it had avoided detection. It had moved around inside the dead woman's brain, wilfully, to avoid the pathologist's probing knife.

Good news: Mystery solved.

Bad news: Bigger mystery now in its place.

Fuck me. This is seriously spooky shit.

She took off a glove and cupped the egg-like thing in her palm. It was warm. Soft. And she could feel it – it was pulsing. Hayley placed the object carefully back on the work surface. She washed her hands in the sink of the autopsy table, rinsing blood off both hands, the bare one and the gloved one. She could see crumbs of brain tissue in the sink. She swallowed. She told herself she wasn't allowed to puke.

Danger turns me on, huh?

It also makes me want to crap myself.

Careful, Hayley, careful.

She plugged in the halogen light and aimed the beam and took a closer look. The tightly focused ray lit the egg-like implant with extraordinary vividness, like headlights dazzling a rabbit. Hayley could see the surface of the 'egg' was marbled, flecked with green and purple. The pulsing was unmistakeable. Hayley could see a shadow inside. The shadow was throbbing, rhythmically; like a pulse. Like a –

An egg.

The egg-like thing actually IS an egg.

What kind of person has an egg in her brain?

Hayley stifled a laugh. By this point, it was more surreal than terrifying.

'You came back to help me. Thank you.'

What?

A whisper; a murmur; like hearing a phone ring two rooms away.

'Thank you so much. Here, I'm over here.'

Hayley turned. The corpse was sitting up on the autopsy table. Its pale face was leering. The top of its skull was missing, creating a flat altar above its staring eyes, like Boris Karloff in the old movies. Its ice-cold dead lips were murmuring to her:

'What's your name, sweetheart?'

Hayley stifled a scream, and took a step back.

Not again!

At that moment she realised that something had happened to the hacked-up brain on the stainless steel work surface. It seemed different somehow. She looked at it more closely. What was different?

It dawned on her that the sections had rejoined. It was now a whole brain again, with scars like painted on lines where the pathologist's knife had cut it up.

Optical illusion?

No, it was real. The slices of brain must have reached out to each other and merged, like jelly voluntarily clambering into a jelly mould.

And now the re-formed brain was shimmering; the pinkish-beige surface of the cortex was trembling. She wondered if it was going to explode, like some kind of comedy brain. Instead, and worse, a stalk of protoplasm shot out of the rear of the cerebrum, the spot where the stub of the spinal cord was located. It was like a tiny pink finger. Or a limb. Then another stalk emerged from further along the brain. The trembling became more intense. More stalks were sprouting out, like eyes on a potato in a damp cupboard, then they were expanding, twitching. And now the stalk-tips were touching the work surface like fingers exploring a lover's body. It was undeniable: the brain was growing legs.

'Speak to me,' said the corpse.

It was a tennis match of horror; what the fuck was she supposed to look at? The talking corpse? Or the animate brain with legs?

Hayley looked at neither; she stared at the floor. 'What you want me to say?' she mumbled, so quietly that even she could barely hear it.

'Tell me your name.'

No!

'I'm Hayley.'

'I'm Jane.'

Hayley tilted her head up a fraction. She was looking at the corpse at an angle now, that made it better somehow.

'You're dead,' Hayley said aggressively.

'It takes a lot to kill my kind.' Its lips were twisted – was it snarling? No, the corpse was smiling, perhaps in an attempt to reassure her.

Don't smile. Please don't smile.

'What exactly is your kind? Who are you? Why are – Fuck,' said Hayley, interrupting herself, as she made a brilliant logical leap.

The brain controlled the body; that's what brains did, right? Hence without its brain the body would die.

And so she grabbed the organ knife; and with a double handed downwards strike, she stabbed the brain. She hacked at it. She ripped off chunks and they spilled on to the floor. And then she smashed the crumbs with the flat of her hand: Bang, bang, bang! The metal echoed. Her hand was damp and sticky with what once had been cells generating thoughts.

'You would do that, to me?' the corpse said, nastily. The scattered brain parts were twitching still, but it was no longer functioning, no longer a whole entity. But that made no difference to the talking corpse. It slid off the autopsy table. It tottered, got its balance. It stared at Hayley. It raised up its dead, cold hands and reached out to her. 'How could you do that to me?' it wailed.

It's going to kill me. It's going to fucking kill me!

Hayley snarled and with knife in hand she lunged at the corpse, intending to gouge the eyes then hack it to pieces.

The half-headed corpse dodged the blow with preternatural speed and grace; and Hayley swung at air and narrowly missed hitting the steel table with the knife.

The corpse took a pace back and assumed a defensive stance, fists clenched. Its dead face could bear no expression, yet it exuded anger. The remainder of its body, naked and icy and utterly sexless, looked like butcher's meat under the pitiless fluorescent light. Snakes of blood were slithering down its neck and shoulders from the burst veins in the face and the eerily flat head.

Time was moving slowly for Hayley. She felt a calm, an ease, that she had never known before, as she computed the next moves in this battle with the undead.

The corpse attacked Hayley with a roar of rage. But Hayley stepped aside. Fists whistled through air; the corpse's punches were powerful and fast. Hayley slashed with the knife and the corpse blocked and the blade dropped out of Hayley's numbed arm.

The corpse threw a punch and Hayley's nose erupted with blood and she fell. The corpse leaped in the air and descended with fists outstretched, to deliver the killer blows.

But Hayley rolled away and leapfrogged over the autopsy table. And took six fast paces and picked up the fire extinguisher, and came running back at the corpse fast and furious.

She hit the creature in the face with the bottom end of the extinguisher. She felt bones crunch. It fell. She hit it again and again, using the extinguisher as a club, until the skull was broken into shards.

But the brainless monster was still alive; it was writhing on the floor.

Oh my god.

The brainless monster stood up. It tried to smile but the bones around its mouth were too badly broken. It held out its palms, like Jesus offering redemption. The lips moved again.

'It's time,' the lips said. But Hayley couldn't understand.

'I'm sorry,' Hayley said 'I didn't mean –'

'My fault. I lost my temper. I got scared. No matter. It's time.'

The creature's lips were reforming. The bones were mending – Hayley could see it happening. The broken nose straightened up. Jane Carter was healing itself.

'It's time.'

This time Hayley understood the words:

'It's time.'

'Time for what?'

Hayley heard a door slam, outside the mortuary. She heard footsteps. 'Someone's coming,' she said.

'It's time.'

'Shit, it's the cops. I –'

'It's –'

Jane Carter was staring at something. Hayley followed her gaze. It was the egg. It had grown to the size of a grapefruit. The marbling had turned pink and ochre and it was throbbing. Then throbbing faster.

It cracked.

It exploded.

But there was no shrapnel; just an explosion of light. Hayley was dazzled. There were spots in front of her eyes, like blood corpuscles. The air around her shimmered and burned. Then the blazing lightshow ebbed and when the air cleared the egg was gone and Hayley was breathing in dank fog. She choked on it. She *ate* it – she drank and chewed thick fog!

A handle rattled. Someone was at the door of the mortuary, which Hayley had bolted from the inside. The door was banged by something hard. It was made of steel and didn't budge. There was a pause. Then the banging resumed. A battering ram or something similar was being smashed against the door.

And finally, Jane Carter's body collapsed. She lay in a sprawled heap on the floor of the dissecting room. She no longer twitched. She no longer spoke. The banging at the door got louder.

Hayley ran. She went out the back door, through the corridor and out of the building. There were cars parked outside the mortuary, she stayed in the shadows to avoid them. They weren't cop cars. Who were they?

Ten blocks away from the hospital she dumped the T-shirt and overalls in a bin.

When she got home she washed off in the shower and when the blood and brains were off her skin and hair, and she was reaching for a towel, she abruptly lost control of her body and fell over in the bathroom. And that's when trembling and the puking and the explosive diarrhoea began.

And, in the midst of the rank shitty trembling horror of it all, she thought: *Fuck. This is it, then.*

I'm dying.

Two

Gwendolyn woke and her body ached. Her hands ached. Her throat was dry. Her eyelids were stiff and hard to open. Her legs were rigid, and every joint throbbed. She felt as if she'd been thrown off a cliff at low tide.

This was how it felt to be old.

She took a light breakfast – orange juice, half a bowl of cereal – and had her morning tablets. The big tablet always made her gag. She'd forgotten, more or less, what the tablets were called, or even what exactly they were for. One was for her heart, she knew that much, one was for her brain. One was for arthritis. The others were – she took them all.

Then she got up for her usual long morning walk, but she had to go to the toilet for a pee first and that added forty-five minutes to her journey. She splashed herself a bit which was mortifying but she'd learned that a little piss on the knickers could be safely ignored, and she wasn't yet ready for incontinence pads. That really was a step too far.

It took her another hour to climb the hillside path. She loved the view of the castle you got from up there. You could see the contours of the old moat, and the ruins of the original Norman walls dotted here and there. The castle itself was mostly Victorian, though Hugh was always ready to debate about which bits were authentic and which weren't. He always claimed to know more than the actual historians who had studied this period. That was Hugh for you.

The morning light was elusively brilliant. The blue sky was scudded with cotton wool clouds.

She could hear the cooing of the wood pigeons above all the other sounds. For her it was even more evocative than the sound of wind through Scotch firs; though, in fairness, that was a sound she had not truly been able to hear for more than twenty years. She could see the greenery stir, but the wind itself had to be deduced. That was age for you. It was stripping her of sensations one tiny step at a time. She couldn't even feel it when she burned herself in the bath water; hence, her trusty thermometer.

Hugh was already at the top of the hill, waiting. She knew how much it vexed him to walk at her slow pace and she'd stopped insisting that he keep her company. She guessed he'd been for a run at dawn. His skin was a ruddy brown. He was braced upon his stick but she knew it was chiefly decorative, on his part. Whereas she needed every bit of the support her two ebony canes gave her.

Her old skin was cold, despite the sun. She focused on locating her centre of gravity, trying to keep her back straight. She knew that if she took a tumble, at her age, bones would break. It happened every now and then and each time the damn bones got more brittle.

There was a sheen of sweat on her wrinkled brow as she heaved up the hill. When she finally reached him Hugh was staring up at the sky.

'Good morning,'

'And good morning to you, my lovely,' he rumbled, gallantly. She gave him a brief smile. That always charmed him. Less now than it did in the old days, when a smile usually promised hours of playful intimacy beneath the sheets. But still, charm was charm, and she did have a shard or so of it left.

They shared the view together, peaceably. Purple heather and rippling mountains. Distant rocky crags shadowed by clouds. A wilderness of Munros that could be ticked off a list yet would always be untamed. Hugh's estate was large as a Western ranch. An expanse of lonely beauty in a land of still lochs and craggy peaks.

She studied his face and saw it light up. She guessed he'd heard something. A helicopter approaching, perhaps.

'Is that Marlowe?' she hazarded.

'It is,' he said. 'Punctual as ever.'

'You won't be tempted back, will you?' Gwendolyn said. 'To the Old Firm, I mean? For "one last job", isn't that what they say?'

'That's what bank robbers say. I was never that, my dear.'

'Well of course not.'

Lady Rothbury – Gwendolyn – had been a great beauty once. Now she was a princess long past her prime. Her grey hair was wispy, her back was crooked. She was almost vulture-like with her Roman nose and skeletal arms. Her perfect face was marred with wrinkles and blotched with liver spots. Her hands were stiff with arthritis, claw-like and undextrous. She was eighty-eight years old and she could, on a good day, so she boasted, pass for eighty-one.

'Oh no, no no, my dear,' Rothbury told her, smiling. 'Those days I fear are long past.' He was two inches taller than her now; she'd shrunk and he hadn't. His hair was grey too; but only because he dyed it. He could run a mile in just under four minutes. His eyesight was perfect. The spectacles, she had realised long ago, were clear glass and just for show.

They'd met when in London at a *soirée*, at a time when evening events were still called *soirées*. She was an heiress and radical feminist of twenty-one years of age, he was a soldier on furlough, and according to his papers he was twenty-five. That meant that now, in the twilight years of their tempestuous yet happy marriage, he had to admit to being ninety-one years old. And yet he still carried himself like an athlete.

Gwendolyn could see the metal bird in the sky now. The thudda thudda thudda swamped the sound of the woodpigeons. There was a patch of flat green on the top of this hillock. The chopper descended on to it, landing with barely a shudder. A chubby, balding man jumped out, wearing a tweed suit and possessed of impeccable poise. He waved, then ducked under the rotors and ran across to them. For a few brief moments he sprinted, like quicksilver slithering across a tray of glass.

But then the balding man slowed, and became visibly out of puff; the walk turned into a waddle. In this fashion Marlowe approached them, as they stood on the summit of a hillside just an arrow's flight from Rothbury's grand castle.

'He's put on a bit of weight,' said Rothbury.

'Indeed,' said Lady Rothbury.

'Hello, Marlowe,' Rothbury said, as the chubby man trudged towards them.

'You look, as always, enchanting, my lady,' Marlowe said gallantly to Gwendolyn. It was heavy-handed flattery but at her age, you took what you got. And so, charmingly, she smiled.

The two men spent the day locked in the old library, hard at work, peered upon by rows of ancient volumes bought by the yard. Every now and then Rothbury would grunt something and Marlowe would take a look. And they would bicker about a minor detail and sometimes tempers would be raised and voices would get louder over a point of principle on which, in fact, they concurred.

The Old Firm was well and truly back.

Rothbury had an old typewriter on which they summarised their notes; the files were then locked in the under-floor safe. Rothbury had never taken to the digital age; he was delighted when, post-Snowden, manual typewriters once again became the tool of choice for the global spy.

At eight they dined. Gwendolyn had authorised the baking of a trout. Moira and Henderson served. Moira wore a demure blue rayon dress with detachable apron and collar. Henderson wore a black morning coat and white wing collar dress shirt. Rothbury was a stickler for such things.

The fish was a giant: Henderson had caught it himself, early that morning. It was one of his many talents. His jacket was bespoke tailored for his needs; you'd have to be an expert to spot the bulge at the back of the coat where he kept his Glock 17.

'Potatoes, Peter?'

'Oh ra-ther,' said Marlowe, in his braying old Etonian voice.

Moira served the potatoes, standing on Marlowe's right-hand side, expertly using fork and spoon like tweezers. Marlowe waited for her to move away then sipped his wine, rosy-cheeked.

'We'll go shooting in the morning, I think,' said Rothbury.

'Jolly good,' Marlowe informed him.

'That old stag, his day has come, I feel,' Rothbury said complacently.

'Surely not,' Gwendolyn interceded.

'He's a magnificent beast.'

'Then let him live.'

'That's not how it works, Lady Rothbury,' Marlowe said.

She yielded the point by pretending there had been no dispute in the first instance.

'But really, Peter,' Gwendolyn said to Marlowe. 'You're too old for these long days of hunting. Especially in this weather. You'll catch your death of cold, you know. And it's been raining, the ground is treacherous.'

'We'll be fine,' Rothbury assured her.

She harumphed, and fixed her husband with a scornful gaze. 'Just take care. You can't afford another fall.'

He shrugged, accepting the scolding in good part. 'I have a stick now,' Rothbury admitted to Marlowe. 'Booked in for a hip replacement.'

'What?' Gwendolyn observed.

Rothbury turned to his wife. 'I'm booked in for a hip replacement.'

'Yes I know that,' she said impatiently.

'I was just telling old Marlowe. He didn't know, you see.'

'Ah, I see. Of course.'

'Age comes to us all, old girl, eh?' Marlowe said reassuringly.

'What?'

'Age comes to us all,' Marlowe explained to her again, over-enunciating.

'Ah yes. True, very true.'

'Also, I've got arthritis in my hands.' Rothbury massaged his hands, wincing.

Gwendolyn was nodding, listening carefully. 'Yes, it's true what he says, I have arthritis in my hands,' she told Marlowe. 'Didn't you have a twinge of it yourself, darling?'

'I did, I had a little twinge,' her husband conceded.

Henderson was there, with impeccable timing, and poured him another glass of the Bordeaux. Rothbury raised a hand; enough. Only half a glass was poured and he sipped it cautiously.

Later the men retired and Gwendolyn fell asleep over her book in the parlour. When she woke she couldn't remember where she was, and when she picked up the book she had no idea what it was about. She placed the bookmark back at the start of Chapter 1 and vowed to try again in the morning.

She rang the bell for Henderson. When he arrived, she couldn't recall why she summoned him. Eventually she said, 'We shall need a new vase for that table.'

The vase on the side table was Edwardian, cobalt blue, and Gwendolyn had always cherished it.

'Yes, my lady.'

'A replica if possible.'

'Yes, my lady.'

Gwendolyn picked up her two sticks and hobbled over to the vase.

'It's older than me, this thing,' she said bitterly.

'Yes, my lady.'

Gwendolyn raised a stick and smashed the vase. She still had some grip in her hand; it was a clean break and made a satisfyingly loud noise. The broken pieces flew, then lay scattered on the Axminster carpet. Henderson didn't flinch but she sensed his disapproval.

'A replica if possible,' said Gwendolyn.

'Yes, my lady, you said, my lady.'

'Did I?'

'You won't tempt me back,' Rothbury lied.

It was quarter past eleven. The two men were in the smoking room. It was Rothbury's favourite room in the house: a club-like den with leather chairs and acres of unread books, crossed swords on one wall, muskets on another, the remaining areas of wall cluttered with barely competent portraits of his ancestors.

'Wouldn't dream of suggesting such a thing,' lied Marlowe.

Ah the old routines.

'How's the port?'

'It's good.'

'I'd say so.'

'How old?'

'A hundred years. I laid it down, oh, well, after that Gibraltar incident,' Rothbury said, remembering.

Marlow shared the memory. It was a terrible memory but time had turned ignominy into a lasting bond.

The smoking room was dimly lit, and the gloom was exacerbated by the sombre colours and cracked chiaroscuro of the Rothbury ancestors. There, above the fireplace, was the 1st Lord Rothbury, who had fought with the Young Pretender. There, his treacherous son the 2nd Earl of Rothbury, who loyally served the Dutch king, and doubled his landownings in Scotland through some clever banking deals. The 3rd Earl of Rothbury built Georgian terraces in London and Bath and tripled the family fortune. The 4th Earl drank himself to death, allegedly, securing a graceful exit from criminal charges being brought against him. The 5th Earl had been a crusty Victorian. The 6th and 7th Earls had served with the Foreign Office and MI6 respectively, and had earned a commendable reputation for their spying skills. The 8th Earl had served his country loyally through the tribulations of the Second World War.

Rothbury was the 9th Earl.

'Brief me,' Rothbury said, after the ports from the decanter had been supped, and cigars had been smoked.

Marlowe nodded and began. His voice was calm, authoritative, sensible. Life, for him, was a series of random facts that cried out to be sifted and turned into order. He had always been so, even as a child.

'The hardliners are in control. Drummond has been appointed as head of the Acronym. He's hardcore, a career soldier, the imagination of a slug. And under his leadership they're eradicating nests in England, Wales and

Scotland. They take no prisoners. They believe in zero tolerance. Frankly, it's carnage, and the enemy are dying in their thousands.'

Rothbury scowling, shaking his head; playing the gavotte of two old-timers returning to their favourite rants.

'Ah, we've seen it all before, Peter, haven't we? It always goes to extremes, for a while. Then the middle way prevails. That's just the way of it.'

'Maybe not this time. The truth is, there aren't many of us left, Hugh. The old guard, I mean.'

'Call me Alan. Please. Otherwise, well. It's hard to keep track.'

'I'm sorry.'

'What about Jane Carter? Was her body retrieved from the mortuary in Leeds?'

'It was.'

'And is she alive?'

Marlowe hesitated, tempted to lie. He knew his old master well.

'Well yes. Astonishingly, she is. She sustained some terrible injuries. There was some kind of – fight.'

'Fight?'

'In the mortuary?'

'Yes, sir.'

'In Yorkshire, they brawl in mortuaries now it seems.'

'She's in intensive care, connected up to a vat of fresh blood.'

'A lot of trouble to go to.'

'The plan is to bring her to trial then execute her.'

'Oh no. What a terrible waste of resources. Bring her to me.'

'To you?'

'That was her intended destination, was it not?'

'I'm not authorised to bring her to you, sir.'

'Do it anyway. Humour me.'

Marlowe had seen this coming; he disapproved but didn't really mind.

'Yes sir.'

'Fake her death, if you have to. Bringing her back to life then executing her! What the hell are these parvenus playing at?'

Marlowe laughed.

'What about the other rogue? Warkworth's steward's boy, wasn't he? Billy Franco?'

'Still on the run.'

'Any other loose ends?'

'One. The lorry driver who crashed into her. It was an accident, but he saw some things at the scene which should not have been seen. And he is considered to be – volatile.'

'How unfortunate. Does he have a name?'

'You don't need to know.'

'Will he be a problem for us?'

'Not any more. He wrote a few blogs, created some questionable hashtags. But nothing serious. He'll soon be forgotten.'

'Forgotten? Are you saying that we –' Rothbury stifled his words. He was no longer the Chief. He had no control over the way things were run.

'I'm sure you will deal with the danger appropriately,' he said.

'Oh, yes, Sir Alan, ra-ther.'

Rothbury tried not to think about the human cost of loose ends.

'My lord,' said Marlowe cautiously, then paused.

'Yes, Marlowe?'

'My lord,' Marlowe said again, and paused again.

'What is it you want me to do, Marlowe?'

'It's time for you to move on, my lord.'

Rothbury made a face. 'Not yet.'

'You need another son.'

'I'm all out of sons.'

'A nephew then, or still better, a great nephew. You need to lose sixty years and rejoin the fray.' Marlowe spoke gently now, prodding at old memories like a man with a stick poking a sleeping tiger. 'The Crusade continues, Sir John, in a new form, and in a new age, and you have your part to play in God's work.'

This time Rothbury didn't correct him.

'I haven't the heart for it,' said Rothbury softly.

'We need you, my lord,' Marlow coaxed.

The consequences of these words were understood clearly by both men. In order to create a new heir, Rothbury's current wife would have to be disposed of. A retirement home was the preferred option in this instance; there Gwendolyn could live out her twilight years. But Rothbury knew she would hate it. And for her, the greatest love of his very long life, he had a soft spot.

'A drop of something stronger?' Rothbury asked.

Marlowe smiled. 'I would be a cur to decline.'

Rothbury led Marlowe across the room, not troubling to use his stick. His companion followed briskly and with a familiar sense of anticipation towards their target: the antique liquor cabinet, made of dark Spanish oak.

Rothbury shuffled through his keys and unlocked the cabinet. He opened up the false back and took out the vials of blood. He poured a vial each into two Waterford brandy glasses.

Then the two men sat in the Robert Adam giltwood chairs on either side of the hearth, occasionally resting their glasses on coasters; feeling like the elegantly debauched Georgian gentlemen that once they were.

'Sláinte'.

'For God and Jerusalem.'

They sipped the blood.

'I agree with you, Drummond and his people, they are zealots,' said Rothbury, continuing their discussion. 'They have no sense of the necessary balance of things. We should – Oh, hello my dear?'

Gwendolyn was at the door. She was flushed and a little drunk. She began walking towards her husband at the far end of the room, her two sticks replacing the power that used to be in her legs. It took a while. The men were unabashed, still sipping blood from their brandy glasses.

'I thought I'd join you,' she puffed.

There was a wild look in her eye which Rothbury knew of old and which he had thought he would never see again.

Marlowe retained a quiet presence, as befitted a man who just a few minutes ago had been plotting to have his hostess incarcerated in an old folks' home so that she might die wretched and alone.

'I know I'm old fashioned,' said Rothbury, bluffly. 'And it's a tradition much in abeyance, for the men to retire separately for their port. But I do feel –'

'Hush, darling. What on Earth is that that you're drinking?'

'Well, port, of course.'

'Liar.'

She still had a few yards to travel. Marlowe stood and offered her his giltwood chair, which she gratefully accepted.

'You eat like a horse, Marlowe,' she told him acidly. 'At dinner you really did pack it away, didn't you?'

'I fear that is the case.'

'And yet you don't savour it. The food I mean. You just eat as if you're obliged to. Furthermore, you've been slim as a rake ever since I met you. How long ago was that? Twenty years? Thirty? So how is it you've suddenly put on so much improbable weight? Are you actually *trying* to get fat?'

'One gets greedier with –'

'It's a clever trick, it makes you look less youthful. Those jowls, that spare tyre you're carrying on your hips. But you have to eat like two men to look even remotely chubby. And the hair.' She raised her stick and waved it at his bald head.

'What little there is of it,' Marlowe joshed.

'I can see the razor rash. You shave your head. You pretend to be bald. Don't you? You're not. You pretend to be fat. You're not. You're as youthful now as you ever – let me taste that.'

'No, ' said Rothbury, coldly.

'And you, you fraud. Arthritis be fucked. Your pubic hair is black, the colour of night. Don't think I don't notice. I look at you, in bed, when you sleep. It's a long time since we – you and – but I still take a peek at what spills out of your Harrods jammies. You've a cock like a horse. The body of a gigolo. You pretend to be old, you're not old. I'm old. I am old. Oh what is this, why all the lies? What are you drinking?'

'Blood.'

'Ah.' Gwendolyn was shocked; though surely it was what she had expected. 'So, we are vampires now, are we?'

'We?'

'Come come come. You can't deny what is self-evident. You're a bloodsucking –'

'I'm not a vampire,' Rothbury said calmly. 'Very well, you may drink the blood.'

She was pleased: mission accomplished. Yet suddenly, existentially, afraid. 'What will it do?'

'It will make you young.'

'Then why didn't you offer it to me –'

Gwendolyn began to weep. Rothbury's heart turned to cracked stone.

'– sooner,' she sobbed.

Rothbury kept his tone calm. 'Because you are not of the Brotherhood. You are not – I don't know, Gwendolyn.'

'She cannot drink the blood, my lord.' Marlowe said sternly. 'We are so pledged.'

'We are pledged, also, to be celibate,' Rothbury chided him, with a wry smile. 'Perhaps it is time we were a little less – narrow minded – regarding our vocation.'

'If that is your decision, my lord, I yield to it,' said Marlowe.

'It is.'

Rothbury stood and took a third glass out of the cabinet and decanted some of his drink into it. A finger, no more; but enough.

'Blood of a virgin?' Lady Rothbury said.

'You are squeamish?'

45

'I have morals.'

'I know you do, my sweet. That is why I allowed you to – get so old.'

'I understand that. I have understood that –' She was weeping again, wheezily, each sob hurt her tiny bird-like chest: '– for many years.'

Rothbury was intrigued. 'When did you realise? That I do not age?'

She laughed. 'Look. Look around you.'

On the walls, stacked like aeroplanes in a holding pattern, were the portraits of the nine generations of Rothbury dating back to the 1st Earl. Rothbury studied them.

'All me,' he conceded.

'So, whose blood is this?'

'Does it matter?'

'Is this a test?'

'Yes.'

'It doesn't matter.'

She took the glass. Her hand was trembling. She took a sip and gagged. It was not port; nor was it meant for drinking. She tried again. She drained it.

'When will it take effect?'

'Not for a while. A few weeks. The effects are cumulative. You should drink a glass a day every month for your first year.'

'And then?'

'And then you will be young. But, dependent.'

'On?'

'On the blood. There must be a continuous flow. No matter what the price, you must have your blood.'

'I see.'

'And it must be aged. Placed in casks, hermetically sealed. It is not safe to drink blood that is less than ten years old. Else the consequences would be – quite terrible.'

'Like wine, you mean? You have to lay it down?'

'Not like wine. Not a bit like wine.'

'I clearly have much to learn.' Lady Rothbury clasped her hands together. Her taking charge gesture. 'Hmmm,' she said slowly as if that were an actual observation.

Then she was silent for a while; both men knew not to interrupt.

'However,' she continued, 'I ask again, now that it is too late for me to step back, now that I am committed – whose blood?'

Rothbury stood. 'Come with me.'

Lady Rothbury couldn't manage the stairs into the basement, so they had to walk back down the side passage then into the secret lift. She braced herself on her sticks and raised her jaw and waited as the lift chundered downwards.

'This takes us to the wine cellar, does it not?'

'To the sub-basement. Below the wine cellar.'

'I didn't know we had such a place.'

'It was a feature of the original Victorian castle. A whole basement level that can only be accessed through secret corridors, or via this concealed pneumatic lift.'

'How enchanting. Hidden dungeons, in effect.'

'That was the architect's fancy.'

The lift stopped, with an unsettling crashing noise. Rothbury slid back the metal grilles. Lady Rothbury stomped out on her sticks, like a spider with four legs.

Down here the air was dense with a wailing sound: incessant, and distressing. Gwendolyn visibly braced herself. Rothbury walked ahead and pulled upon the stem of a gas lantern. The stem moved downwards, the sheer brick walls facing them slid slowly apart.

'Very droll.'

'This house is a sublime folly; that's why I love it so.'

Rothbury walked through the opening first, followed slowly by Gwendolyn with Marlowe taking up the rear; and as he entered Rothbury switched on a set of wall-mounted gas lamps which flickered dimly and turned Stygian night into visible nightmare.

Beyond the concealed entrance was a huge cellar the size of a rock cavern with black brick walls and old stone pillars; and scores of emaciated men and women were chained to the walls, semi-clad for the most part, many with fabric pooled at their feet where their clothes had rotted off with age. They were connected by thin IV tubes to huge glass vials of blood; each of them blinking as the yellow light dazzled their eyes. From them the wailing emanated, like a tidal wave slowly travelling between continents, betokening endless pain.

'These are our prisoners?' Gwendolyn was truly shocked now, but she was too much of a lady to reproach her husband for keeping a dungeon full of starving slaves.

'We think of them as guests.'

'Are they free to go?'

'No.'

'Then they are prisoners.'

He conceded the point. 'We bleed them every day, to keep them weak.

It gives us more blood than we need but when they are strong, they are really very strong.'

'What if one of them escaped?'

'They couldn't escape. It's not – it's never happened.'

Gwendolyn peered, tears in her eyes.

'They are in such pain. It's like – this is truly disgusting, Hugh. It's not right.'

'These creatures are not human. They have no rights. '

'Devils?'

'Hardly. They are from – another place.'

'Which other place?'

'Far far away.'

'Just say it, for Christ's sake.'

'Another planet,' Rothbury told her.

The wailing noise continued, unabated, like white noise; it was horrendous.

'Planet?' The word was said; the truth was known. She absorbed its implications.

'This is what you must endure, if you wish to join me.'

She nodded, firmly. 'I can endure this.'

Three

Hayley opened her eyes and Liam was smiling down at her.

'That must have been a hell of a night last night,' she groaned.

He was still smiling.

'What time is it?'

'Four o'clock.'

'I slept till four?'

'You've been asleep for three days, honey.'

Hayley woke up. She was in a big double bed. Ruched curtains. Wearing pyjamas. She never wore pyjamas.

'Where am I?'

'My place.'

'How did I get here?'

'Wrapped in a blanket. Took two of us to get you out. Boy, Hayley, when you fuck up you really fuck up.'

'I passed out?'

'You've been missing for three days. I had to kick in the door of your flat. The smell was – oh my God. You must be crazy.'

'Yeah one crazy chick, that's – three days?'

'What was it? Heroin?'

''Huh?'

'You went cold turkey on your own. Was it heroin?'

'I don't want to talk about this.'

'If so, where are the needle marks?'

'I'm so not talking about this.'

Memories were coming back. The mortuary. The walking brain. The woman with the smashed in head. The egg exploding, the fog in her throat, choking her, filling her entire body with its dank presence...

Staggering home and collapsing in the bathroom. All the disgusting stuff that followed. She had left her clothes in the bath and crawled into bed. Then she had dreamed.

'You saved my life,' she said.

'Pretty much.'

'Does Cheyney know?'

Terrible terrible dreams.

'Of course she knows! You think I'm not going to tell her that her sister almost died? You can't do that shit on your own, Hayley. You should have had a babysitter. Or checked into a clinic. I'd have paid.'

She gave Liam a hate-filled glare. 'I don't want your fucking money.'

'You're better off taking my fucking money than drowning in your own vomit, darling,' he said, mildly.

Oh shit. I've missed –

'The wedding. I missed the wedding.'

Liam shook his head.

'I didn't miss the wedding?'

'We postponed it a week.'

'You can't do that.'

'We did that.'

'But it's all booked – it would cost a fortune to –'

'I'm good for it. Me with all my fucking money, remember. My ill-gotten gains.'

Hayley was furious. He wasn't even embarrassed about it!

Liam was a career criminal. It wasn't just a rumour – all the crime reporters knew his rep, and they wrote regular features about him as if he was a local celebrity. Armed robber. Loan shark. Dodgy property deals. Hayley despised him for it. But no one seemed to *care* – good looking Irish bloke, lots of money to throw around, what was the problem? But for Hayley it was all wrong. Her baby sister deserved better than this – fucking *– gangster.*

'Shit, you would do that, for me?' Hayley said.

'Cheyney would.'

'I feel so bad.'

'Don't feel bad.'

'Why not?'

'Okay then, feel bad.'

'I feel shit.'

Not my fault! I'm not a junkie! I didn't go cold turkey! And it's not my fault that I was infected by – infected by – infected by –

She realised, it was better to admit to being a junkie that try to explain all *that* stuff.

'I'm hungry.'

'So am I. Let's go eat.'

Billy watched them leave the Irishman's house. He waited until they were out in traffic then eased out of his parking space. He kept his car as far away as he could, with five or six vehicles between them. The Irishman was a careful driver, his signalling was good, so Billy had no trouble keeping up.

The car was stolen, Billy was adept at that. And he guessed he had three or four hours before he'd have to ditch it and find a clean vehicle. He'd robbed an ATM two nights ago by ripping it out of the wall, which was risky but he had no contacts here. No ID. No legal way of accessing cash. Jane had always had a knack of getting money out of men in expensive hotel rooms, but Billy couldn't face the idea of whoring himself, and he didn't know how to bribe the concierges. He was lost without her.

And afraid.

Billy was used to being afraid. In some ways he found it comforting when he was in pain or being tortured, because then there was nothing to be afraid of – the worst was already happening. But when he was free, and safe, fear consumed him. An unceasing low level panic that was worse, well, than being buried under a mountain of plague-infested bodies.

As a boy, Billy had been feisty and fearless. A peasant lad who would say anything to anyone. But the more his 'powers' had grown, the more fearful he had become.

Jane had tried to explain to him why this was so. She told him their kind were two distinct beings in one body. There was the human Billy and the other Billy. The human Billy didn't give a shit, you couldn't scare *him*. But the other Billy, the immortal Billy, that was where the fear came from.

Jane was bolder than he was. But even she felt it – the oppressive presence of an immortal creature in her body and her mind that was sentient, but not truly 'conscious'. A hive-mind entity that would not fight and would not build, and loved nothing and cared for nothing, but was blindly and fearfully determined to survive.

A parasite, in other words.

Parasites by their very nature are exploiters. They are thieves which lurk in or upon their host body and pillage and destroy. They do not stand

and fight; they do not know *how* to fight. And when they kill they do so slyly and thoughtlessly. Usually by bursting out of their host creature's body in a variety of appalling ways.

Billy knew these truths about himself: he was a parasite and a coward and he was not able to defend himself and the people he loved.

But now his wife was dead, her remains taken away (or so he presumed) by the DOH. And he knew the identity of the killer. For he had been told it, by the best eyewitness possible – Jane Carter herself.

On that evening, the evening Jane had died, Billy had arrived at the hospital at about five in the morning. There he found that the doors had been forced open. When he went inside, he sensed that a battle had taken place in the mortuary, and he could see that some of the jars and test tubes had been smashed. The floors and surfaces had been thoroughly cleaned, but even so he could detect tiny shards of her brain in the sink, and on the wall. And when he went out of the back entrance of the mortuary he could smell her there; microscopic particles of her alive in gobbets of oxygenated blood, somewhere nearby.

And so he'd spent the next hour hunting for her blood, like a dog searching for a scrap of buried meat. And then he'd found it: a bloodied T-shirt and bloodied plastic coverall, thrown into a rubbish bin. Rich in the aroma of the one he had loved. And when he breathed in her scent, rich in her signalling molecules, she came alive again. For just a moment; a few precious moments.

And thus Billy had inhaled the last few shreds of life in the blood of Jane Carter, his beloved wife.

And then he knew everything. The pain of her post mortem. Her attempts to communicate with the woman in the mortuary. And her subsequent brutal murder.

Billy could remember the scene as vividly as if he had been there himself. The crazed face of the woman with the purple hair and the tunnel piercings and the mad staring eye, hacking at Jane's brain, slashing her body, then smashing her skull to pieces with a fire extinguisher. And, finally, taking away the last living remnants of Jane away on the T-shirt: the droplets of blood that contained the sentient essence of the parasitical entity that had once co-existed with the soul and mind of his wife.

Then the blood on T-shirt staled, and Jane passed on to nowhere. There was no afterlife for parasites.

And Billy was left with nothing but his own anger. Burning rage at what this vicious purple-haired woman had done, her cruel slaughter of his wife and unhatched egg.

Yet what should he do now? Seek out the purple-haired woman and wreak his vengeance? Kill her? Or torture her, so she had time to repent of her cruelty, and *then* kill her?

Just the thought of such a decisive action made him twitch with terror. His kind could not comprehend revenge. They had not evolved to hunt and kill. They just stole whatever they could, by whatever means were at their disposal.

They were like the nematode that gestates in the body of a pregnant mayfly and then explodes out of its abdomen, ripping the creature apart.

They were like the *Sacculina* parasite that fills the body of its host crab, wrapping its roots around the creature's eyeballs.

They were like the guinea worms that hatch their eggs in a woman's uterus, then crack the womb, and create burning lesions to make her seek cooling water; before finding their escape route out of her body into the water, through her vomit.

And in many ways, they were most akin to Earth's most prevalent parasite, the virus; that ever-mutating shred of life that infects its host and subverts its immune system, turning a living creature into a walking foodstore.

But now, defying his own biology, his own genetic legacy, the young man with the ponytail felt a terrible rage sweep over him.

He sat parked outside the greasy spoon where Hayley and the Irishman were laughing and chatting – watching them through the plate glass windows. And he made a solemn vow to the memory of his wife and their unborn child.

I will make her pay, my love. I vow it. That evil bitch shall die in pain and torment for what she did to you.

'Boy, you can eat,' said Liam, marvelling.

Hayley was on her third cooked breakfast. Hollow legs, was what her Mam used to call it. But she didn't feel bloated. She felt fresh. Alert. Two men at another table were watching them, covertly, and Hayley guessed they knew Liam by repute.

'Are you paying for this?'

'Do you have money on you?'

'Nah.' Hayley was wearing clothes that Liam had foraged from her wardrobe. She realised that he, or someone, must have stripped her and wased her. The thought gave her a tingle, but not a good one.

'Then I'll pay. You don't like me much, do you?'

'Why would I not like you? You're the evil thieving bastard who's going to break my sister's heart.'

'Ah, now there you're wrong.'

'She told me you weren't having a stag night.'

'We did agree that, yes,' said Liam, taken aback.

'But you did have a stag night, didn't you?'

'Course not!'

'You and a bunch of mates, getting pissed, drinking till the early hours in Red Leopard dancing with the lapdancers. That's what I heard.'

Liam was shocked. 'Who the hell told you about that?'

Hayley hid a smile. 'No one. I guessed.'

Liam's face flickered: she'd well and truly got him there.

'My brothers insisted,' Liam admitted, ruefully. 'Rite of passage. I couldn't let them down, now, could I?'

'So you lied to my sister, then committed adultery a week before her wedding?'

'Two weeks before, as it happens, counting this delay which is entirely your fault, and I didn't commit adultery. I just – watched.'

'Same thing.'

'Yeah but she had strippers at her hen night!' Liam protested.

'She did not!'

'She did. I got a full report on that one.'

Hayley thought back. She'd been there, she knew that much. The rest was a blank.

'That's different, when girls do it it's a laugh.'

'I didn't commit adultery,' said Liam softly. 'I know what you think about me. It's mostly true. I'm one hard bastard and I've an eye for the ladies. But those days are done.'

'You're a changed man, are you?'

'You could say that.'

'Doesn't happen. No one changes. Once a bastard, always a bastard.'

'No one changes. You really believe that?'

Hayley thought about it. 'No.'

'So what you really think is, *you* might be able to change, but not me?'

'I don't need to change.'

'You might consider getting off the heroin and not being such a foul-mouthed bitch, maybe.'

'Who said I'm a foul-mouthed bitch?'

'Well I just did.'

'Well –' Hayley silently mimed the lyrics of the filthiest rap song she knew. Liam could lip-read well enough; he grinned.

Hayley finished her plate and mopped the sauce up with some white bread. She still felt hungry.

She realised she was happy. Liam was smiling at her indulgently.

'Take me home, please?'

'Sure.'

'Is it –?'

'I had the place fumigated.'

'Oh you kiss-arse! Is there no limit to what you'll do to make my sister happy?' Hayley goaded.

'Not really. And I didn't do it for her, I did it for you, you daft bitch.'

Hayley had no comeback.

It was three blocks from the pub to the target's house.

Earlier that day, at 7.05pm, DOH surveillance teams had followed him from the house to his local, using long lenses and a mobile phone hack. The photos had been sent to Control to confirm the identity of the target. A search team had broken in and fingerprinted the kitchen utensils to double check that this individual definitely was Tony Riley, lorry driver.

You can't be too careful, with wetwork.

At 7.35pm, an undercover agent wandered into the pub for a quick half of pale ale and had lingered to monitor the target's consumption. The agent had observed that the target was a solitary drinker, and a heavy one, consuming three pints of Doombar in the hour the agent was there.

Web intercepts had shown that the target was a late night obsessive blogger with a tendency to flame his enemies whilst drunk. So two days previously, at Marlowe's instructions, a cut out had been created to divert all his internet traffic to a site in Germany, where a team of highly paid geeks were masquerading as conspiracy theorising trolls.

All the evidence suggested that the target was a strange man. He was an IT specialist who had been sacked from a pretty good job for antisocial behaviour, and had taken to HGV driving as a second career choice. He drove lorries of cigarettes across Europe, he never socialised with the other drivers, he was reliable to a fault but not well liked.

Hence, he wouldn't be missed.

A team of ten wetworkers had been assigned to the job, with full logistical support. Money was never an object for the DOH.

The oldest assassin was twenty-nine, but all of the team could pass for teenagers. They were all born into supreme wealth and none of them needed to work for a living. All the men were educated at Eton, the two women hailed from Cheltenham Ladies College.

Tonight they were pretending to be Yardie-affiliated gangstas, and were skilfully made up to look their parts, like a gang of psychopathic Black and White Minstrels.

They lay in wait on the pavement between the pub and the target's home, in a blatant druggie huddle, swapping 'innits' and 'bloods', and 'feeling clappin' man' and 'dreds' and 'fucking feds' and 'merks', in a preposterous medley of memorised rap lyrics, until the target emerged from the pub and walked towards them. Then they moved in.

'Give us your raasclat phone, man, innit!' cried one young Etonian.

'Huh? What?'

They kicked the target to death. It took a while. Their boots had steel plates in the toes and strengthened heels. The first kick shattered the target's larynx, to prevent him screaming. The kickers were shielded from view by two semicircles of loitering youths; from a distance, it looked as if drugs were being bought or sold. When he was confirmed as dead they took his phone. They took his wallet too, though there wasn't much cash in it. The cards would be melted and the leather would be burned, later.

The lorry driver died not knowing why he had to die. He was a dyed-in-the-wool conspiracy theorist but even he wasn't *that* paranoid.

Careless words. Words he should never have said:

'A mist of blood, dancing, in front of her – her body, then she opened her mouth and sucked and the blood flew up into the air and she drank it in. Drank her own blood.'

Witnesses later reported that a gang of black youths wearing hoodies had fled the scene where a local man was beaten to death for his mobile phone.

Marlowe was pleased. Two Actions resolved. The body of Jane Carter retrieved. And Tony Riley, TWP. All that was left was for them to dispose of the purple-haired girl from the mortuary.

And after that –

Marlowe had loved the old days. He hated these new days, and he hated Drummond and his kind. He hated the guns and the mobile phones and the written reports and the performance appraisals that even he – he! – had to endure these days. But he had now been assured that, within the next few weeks, Rothbury would rejoin the fray. Rejuvenated, re-energised, inspirational.

My Lord, I shall serve thee to the end of my days.
Rothbury was a true knight, one of the few to live up to the ideals of their Sacred Order, and Marlowe had once been his squire.

Together they had conquered Jerusalem. And Marlowe's hope was that – metaphorically – they would now be able to do so again.

Hayley stared at her mother as she approached the Hebden Bridge Town Hall, looking like a multi-coloured dirigible.

Acting upon very specific orders from her younger sister, Hayley forced a big smile on to her face.

'Wake up, Mam. Wake up.'
Mam stirred. She snored. She shifted her bulk on the sofa. Hayley didn't want to be late for school. But she didn't want to leave her mother like this.

'Are you okay, Mam?'
A snore, a grunt. Mam was always okay. She had amazing survival instincts.

Hayley went to the bathroom with a washing up bowl and filled it and stirred in some soap, then she came back and mopped her mother's face with a flannel. She'd clearly fallen down drunk somewhere, there were scabs on her face and her hands. Hayley cleaned them and disinfected them with a wipe then dried them carefully with a hand towel. When she was finished she gave her mother a kiss on the cheek. Her little message to say, 'I'm always here for you.'

But Mam didn't feel it and if she'd felt it she wouldn't have remembered it. And that afternoon when Hayley came home from school Mam was baking cakes and scones with Cheyney and the two of them were chattering and gossiping and it was as if Hayley didn't exist.

That was then. This was now.
Still with the big smile etched on her face, Hayley strode towards her mother like a heat-seeking missile. She held her tongue till she was too close to be ignored, then launched into it:

'All right, Mam!' Hayley almost shouted. 'How are you then? Wonderful weather for a wedding, isn't it, and oh that dress is lovely!' Over-rehearsed hardly covered it, but at least no one could say she wasn't saying the right things.

Mam did a double take. Looked her daughter up and down.

Stared at her tunnel piercings and her flat breasts, like a sergeant major doing a kit inspection on Dennis the Menace. Her disdain was almost palpable.

Are you really so ashamed of me, Mam? Am I really such a terrible daughter?

They were standing outside the entrance of the Town Hall, amid a swarm of wedding goers all in their best glad rags. The weather was in fact lovely and above her richly coloured dress Mam was wearing a big white hat tinted with yellow nicotine stains.

'Smashing, eh!' Hayley added, hoping that today of all days things would be different between her and her Mam.

They weren't.

Mam followed up her startled double take with a weary glance. A fuck off and die before you disappoint us yet again look.

'Try not to bugger up your sister's wedding, eh? Or is that too much trouble?' she said eventually, then sucked at her fag. Despite her formidable bulk, and her shockingly unhealthy lifestyle, Mam exuded energy and life force. She was like three people rolled into one. That's why everyone loved her.

'Course I won't. I mean it's not.' Hayley felt herself babbling.

Mam blew smoke rings in the air: a lost art. The three page boys in their cute three piece suits looked goggle-eyed at that.

Mam adopted a stage whisper, audible streets away: 'I hear you OD'd. I hear Liam found you in a pile of your own puke and shit, like.'

'That's not exactly what happened.'

'What happened then?'

'Long story.'

'Jesus! Heroin! A child of mine, on heroin! The shame of it. If your father was alive today, well, let's spare him the shame.'

Hayley's dad had scarpered when Hayley was two years old; no one knew if he was alive or dead.

'Yeah but you're a bloody prescription pill addict and alcoholic, and my granddad had a nervous breakdown because of you,' Hayley wanted to tell her mother. Because all of those things were true. But she didn't say any of it.

'Just don't fuck up or have a seizure or anything, oh, and what's wrong with your legs? Why are you wearing curtains?' Mam said, in shocked tones, and those were the last words she spoke to Hayley all day long.

'I, Cheyney Patricia Bradley, take you to be my lawfully wedded husband. Before these witnesses I vow to love you.'

The service was being held in the Council Chamber. The registrar sat at a magohany desk, her back to the guests. The bride stood proudly, Uncle Mack on one side of her, Liam and ex-getaway driver Best Man on the other.

Mam stole the show, with her multi-coloured billowing dress and her ridiculous hat and her girth. She had taken upon herself the right to give her daughter away, in the absence of Cheyney and Hayley's dad.

'And now it's your turn,' said Cheyney to Liam. 'Come on love, can't back out now.'

Liam grinned. He was bursting out of his grey morning suit, an unexpected silver earring in his left ear. He kissed the bride, ahead of schedule, gave her a little pat on her arse, and she kissed him back.

Cheyney's dress hugged her where it mattered before pooling into a lake of red fabric below the bustle. She was sexy beyond belief, in Hayley's humble opinion. The bridesmaids were gowned fussily in rose-pink. All three of them were slim and gorgeous and moved in easy unison; they could have been the backing singers to Cheyney's Shakira.

Liam gave it his all: 'I, Liam Maloney, take thee Cheyney Patricia Bradley, to be my awfully –' Pause, grin, the lads loved that: '*lawfully* wedded wife. To have and to hold –'

'Read the card, Liam.'

Liam read the card: 'Before these witnesses I vow to love you –'

Hayley kept staring at her Mam.

'And I really do love you, petal. You are the light of my life,' Liam said, ad-libbing.

Everyone laughed at that, except Hayley.

Not the hospital for stupid children, *again.*

You really are a waste of space, Hayley.

Hello, Mam, can you see me? I'm standing right in front of you? I'm here, it's my sister's wedding, I'M HERE!

'Hayley, you coming?'

It was all over, apparently.

'Yeah yeah yeah.'

Hayley was the last to leave the Council Chamber. The sunshine that had followed the morning's rain poured through the windows. Dust motes hovered.

Then it was canapés and Walker's crisps on the Terrace, overlooking the rushing waters of the Rochdale Canal.

'Great wedding, eh ?' someone asked her.

And yeah, it was. Except, Hayley had a stone where her heart should be.

A waiter was standing at her shoulder. She glanced at him. Then glanced again. He was cute. Young, muscular, good looking if you liked that sort of thing, which Hayley (shamefacedly) did. His hair was scrunchied into a ponytail. He wore a short-sleeved shirt and his arms were decorated with tattoos – Frank Sinatra on one arm, Grace Kelly on the other. Adorably retro.

Hayley raised her head when he filled her wine glass, so he could spot the blue butterfly tat under her chin. The one weird thing about her that most people didn't tend to notice. He did notice. He smiled.

'Like the hair,' he murmured, flirtily.

She'd taken the lime-green highlights out of her purple hedge, and she had to admit it worked a hell of a lot better that way.

'Hmm, yeah, right,' she said ungraciously.

'Are you here for the bride or the groom?'

Oh my God, are you chatting me up? Sorry, pal, but do you not know who I am? That I am a pariah in this community?

'Um.'

'The bride?'

'Um.' He took that as a yes.

'She's my sister,' Hayley added. She was staring at his face, which was lovely.

He reached over and stroked her hair.

'Sorry, you had a –'

'What?'

'Thing. Just there.'

'Cobweb?'

'Bit of fluff. Maybe some cherry blossom. '

He opened his hand. There was a cherry blossom cupped in his palm. 'Yeah, that's what I thought.' He threw it in the air; the air caught it. The pink cherry blossom hovered for a brief instant on invisible currents of air, then was gone.

The waiter moved on. She followed him with her eyes.

Well why shouldn't I?

She checked out again the tat on his right arm, the Grace Kelly. No, she was wrong about that, it was a woman with blonde hair holding a guitar. Who though? She peered. Dirty Jenny? Orianthi? It was definitely a blonde rock guitarist NOT a blonde screen siren in a white dress. Odd, thought Hayley, how could she have been mistaken about that?

'Look at her!' Cheyney was at her shoulder, still in her scarlet hussy dress.

'At her age – she's amazing!' Cheyney said cheerfully. Hayley rubbed her front teeth over her tongue, holding back the sark.

Cheyney was looking at Mam. Their mother had taken off her hat, and also her shawl, revealing her beefy upper arms. She was talking animatedly to a pal of Liam's, Hayley didn't know his name, but he was twenty-five at most and looked like the guy who played Thor.

And he was laughing at her jokes! Lapping her up, in fact. Mam was forty-five years old, three stone away from being morbidly obese, pickled in booze, hooked on prescription pills, addicted to life on benefits; but she still had it.

Looking at her, Hayley wanted to weep.

'Bless her,' said Cheyney, who had a heart of gold.

'She's on something.'

'She's just happy.'

Mam leaned across the table, tilting her head towards Liam's gym-ripped pal. Gym-Boy took the hint, and leaned over and kissed her gently on the cheek. Then less gently, on the lips. As they kissed, Mam cupped Thor's head with four strong fingers and a thumb hardened by years of operating the remote control. She wasn't, it seemed, going to let him go.

Hayley was stunned. Gross hardly covered this nightmare scenario.

'You look, um, great, Chey,' Hayley said, weakly.

Cheyney dragged her stare away.

'Thanks.'

'Love you,' Hayley said.

'What?'

'Love you.'

Cheyney laughed at that. 'Fuck me. You'll be crying in chick flicks next.'

'I don't fucking think so.'

'That's my girl.' And Cheney beamed, radiating joy. 'Try and score, love, eh? Lots of Liam's mates around. They're not fussy, I mean, look at Mam. Even a dog like you should manage a shag by the end of the evening.'

Cheyney bustled off.
Hayley slowly smiled.

Hayley drank six glasses of free Cava then cracked and went to the pay bar and bought a pint of Tetley's.

Liam joined her. Grinning like he owned the place, rather than just renting it by the hour.

'All right, Hayley, love. How are you doing?'

'I'm fine.'

Ah yes. You saw me naked in a mountain of my own shit and vomit. But let's pretend that never happened, hmm?

'Enjoying yourself?'

She thought about that, too much. 'Yeah, s'pose.'

'You don't look it.'

'Fuck off, Liam.'

He grinned. 'You're a charmer, you really are.'

She hesitated. She was not a gracious person by nature, she prided herself on that. But even for her, there were limits.

'Thank you for, you know. All that you did,' she said shyly.

It had been without doubt the most harrowing experience of her entire life. But she was successfully managing not to think about any of it. Denial, it seemed, wasn't always such a bad thing.

Liam gave her a strange look.

'No worries,' he said cheerfully. 'Any time. Well no – never again. You know what I mean.'

He was towering over her, leaning down a bit to make it easier for her to talk to him.

'Enjoy yourself, right? That's an order. '

'I'll try.'

And that was it: Liam was gone.

She drained her Tetley's. Long night ahead.

'Good to see you, sir,' said Smith.

'At ease, sergeant.'

Smith relaxed not a jot. Marlowe smiled.

A good man. In other words, a man you would want by your side in battle. A total shit of course. But aren't we all?

They were in the Brewery Tap, the Upstairs Bar. Four or five other tables were occupied by groups of two or three or four; all of them working for Marlowe.

Marlowe had had a busy few days covering up the Jane Carter abduction. Smith and his men had taken her corpse, or what remained of it, to a secure storage unit. Marlowe ordered a comprehensive set of photos of the body and sent them to Drummond and closed the case file on CARTER, JANE ALLISON NÉE LADY URSULA WARKWORTH: DECEASED.

In fact she was still alive. Astonishingly. Her blood pumped even though her heart was in shreds. Her mind was still active, even though it was no longer supported by an organic brain. These creatures! Marlowe marvelled at their tenacity.

Then, following orders, Marlowe packed the mess of a body into an ambulance and had her driven north to the Chief. The old man could pick the last shreds of goodness from the monster's blood.

Marlowe sipped a pint of ale.

'Will you join me, sergeant?'

'No sir. I never drink on duty, sir.'

Ah you bloody lightweight! We always drank on duty, back in the day. When we stormed Jerusalem, there wasn't a sober man in the regiment.

'So tell me about the mortuary woman,' instructed Marlowe.

'She's away for the weekend, as it happens. Out in the country. Wedding.'

'When?'

'Tonight. Now in fact.'

'Do you have a team in place?'

'Yes, sir. We have a disposal team on standby and two agents on surveillance duties. One posing as a guest, the other as a waiter working for the catering company.'

'Good man.'

'They report that Bradley is drinking heavily. Scuttlebutt suggests she has a rep for being a piss-head and also a heroin addict.'

'Even better.'

'Hence, our strategy will be to send a team into her room at the B&B, and persuade her to choke on her own vomit.'

'Very good. Make it happen.'

Smith sent the email. Encrypted, buried in a routine spam message; hard to trace back to his phone. A ping marked the imminent death of

Hayley Bradley.

'And what about Jane Carter's husband?' Marlowe asked. 'William Prentis aka Billy Franco?'

'No trace of him as yet, sir,' said Smith.

Hayley was in the Waterfront Hall at her designated table. She was pissed. Starters had been served, when the fuck did *that* happen? Hayley realised she'd skipped half an hour.

Okay, here's the challenge; I look up at the ceiling. If it moves, I'll stop drinking.

She looked at the ceiling. It moved.

She drained her pint and started on the next.

The sexy waiter was there again, standing close to her.

'More wine?'

'I'm on the beer,' she said, gesturing at the cluster of pints she had assembled around her.

'I'll get you a whisky chaser, if you like.'

'Can't afford it, it's a pay bar.'

'I'll buy you a drink. You don't need to steal other people's left-overs.'

He was smiling at her.

He's laughing at me.

Don't you fucking laugh at me, you fucking prick!

Laugh at me if you like, I don't fucking care.

God, you're sexy.

A tat of Daenerys Targaryen flowed down his bare left arm, her white hair vivid against his tanned skin.

Fuck, I really am drunk. I'm sure that wasn't –

'We could go somewhere,' suggested the waiter.

'Speeches,' Hayley hazarded, 'coming soon.'

'Not till after pudding. And service is crap here, it's gonna be half an hour till your main course. Come on, I need to talk to you before you pass out.'

'What about?'

'Just come with me.'

She followed him out of the hall. Into the corridor, paintings of blue sky all down the wall, like portholes on a ship.

Up a set of stairs. She was sobering up, fast. She exhaled twice, three times. She wondered what was going on.

Hey, maybe I'm in here!

Dream on, you idiot.

The waiter walked up to the second floor, then turned right. He tried the first door he came to. She arrived just as he raised a foot and kicked the door in.

'Hey.'

'S'okay. Don't sweat it.'

She felt a twinge of panic. 'What the – what the hell is this about?'

'We have to talk.'

She followed him into the room. It was an office, not for use by guests. The waiter turned around and raised a finger to his lips.

'Are you trying to rape me or something?"

'No!' He was shocked. 'Of course not.'

Nice one, Hayley.

'I'm sorry, awful thing to say, I didn't mean to –'

'You desire me, don't you?' he said, amused. 'I can smell it on you, the pheromones, the –' He broke off.

'No, course I don't – You cheeky bastard! What makes you think –?'

Course I bloody do. I fancy the fuck out of you.

The waiter was staring at her strangely. He sniffed her. Then again, as if she had chronic BO or something.. Rude!

He began to take his shirt off.

What! Stop it!

Christ he's gorgeous.

This is SO wrong, it's my sister's wedding!

The shirt came off. He threw it on the floor. He was impressively muscular, and his upper body was as richly decorated as an oriental carpet. Interlocking tattoos of gods and mythological creatures were carved upon his naked flesh. Beautiful sirens; a white winged stallion; a blue and grey manticore; two golden griffins; a trio of black-haired shikagami. His body was a Sistine Chapel of the inker's art.

She felt a surge of hot, needy, liquid lust.

'Look closer.' He gestured, brusque rather than seductive.

She stepped forward and stared at his pectorals which bore the white winged stallion, wings spanning ample breasts of pure compacted muscle. He twitched his pectorals and the wings flapped.

'Are you gay?' Hayley taunted.

But then the wings flapped again. And the stallion moved; it slithered off its fleshly perch, then flapped down his body, along his taut abs and down to the belly button. Then it morphed and became a snake, its jaws wide open beneath its hood, baring fangs and a red bifurcated tongue.

A moment later, and the cobra slithered back up his naked torso, undulating over the other mythological creatures. The waiter's skin was gleaming with sweat, as if the snake were leaving a trail of slime.

She was impressed. 'Hell of a trick, I'll grant you that,' she informed him. 'You should go on the –'

The snake vanished; leaving smoke in the air. The other tats swirled, as if hit by a typhoon of soot, then once more formed a shape. The shape was a face. A woman's face. A beautiful woman's face with raven-black hair. The face of Jane Carter, who had died twice in the last week; the first time in a car crash, the second time when her brain and skull were smashed to pieces by Hayley.

'Remember her?'

'Not sure.'

Oh no.

'Don't lie to me. This is my wife, Jane Carter. Do you know her?' he said again.

Hayley was too confused to lie. 'Yes.'

'How?'

'She came to my mortuary. I work – in a mortuary.'

'Was she dead when she came to your mortuary?'

'Yes. No. She –'

'What?'

'Spoke to me?'

His expression darkened, forebodingly.

'Show me your tattoo. That one there.'

He was pointing at the large Celtic Cross on the arm that didn't have the map of Terra Incognita. In memory of her Nan who was Irish.

Hayley looked at the Cross. It was understated, by her standards, but she was fond of it.

'Make it into a flower.'

'What?'

'Visualise a flower. Think it. Be it. Then make the Cross a flower.'

'This is – what, are you like Dynamo? He's a Northerner too, isn't he?'

'I'm not a conjurer. Look at the tat. Think flower.'

Hayley stared at the Celtic Cross inked on the skin of her arm.

A flower. What sort of flower?

She couldn't think of any flowers, so Hayley just visualised a generalised flower, green stalk and yellow blossom.

A daffodil?

Nothing happened.

'Persist.'

Nothing happened.

'Persist.'

'I am persist –' The ink on her skin swirled. The Celtic Cross on her flesh shook and crumpled and collapsed into a blob. Then it sprang up again, making the skin ripple. A new tattoo was formed. The upright bar of the Cross was now a green stalk. A splurge of yellow blossomed above it on her inner arm. Green stick, yellow blob. It wasn't a flower it was a mess. But the point was proven.

'Wow. That's even better. To do it to me! It's a really good trick.'

'It's not a trick,' he said impatiently. 'You just – it's to do with the melanin in your body. Naturally occurring pigments, merging with the tattoo ink, becoming one. It's about controlling your body, as we do. As we all do. As Jane did, when she spoke to you, when she begged you to help her and to save her child.'

Hayley was stone cold sober now; improbable but true.

'How did you know about that?' she said cautiously.

He shrugged.

'I'm lost,' Hayley said helplessly. 'Who are you? What are you? How can you do these things?'

'Jane and I, we are not – not like other people.'

'Mutant, you mean?'

'No. Not exactly.'

'What then?'

'Not from Earth.'

Ah, yeah, right, that explains it.

'Alien, you mean.'

'If that's what not from Earth means to you, then yes. '

'What,' Hayley said, in tones of withering scorn, 'are you saying your spaceship crashed, and you couldn't get back to your home planet?'

'Pretty much,' he said.

Her face fell. Her sarcasm sounded, even to herself, like stupidity.

'I don't believe you,' she floundered.

'It happened,' said Billy Franco. 'A long time ago. More than a thousand years, ago. At the dawn of the second millennium. In all that time we have lived among humans. And now –'

'What?'

What?

'You don't get it yet, do you? The tattoo. What you did. It was the same as what I did. The same – power. Don't you see? Don't you get it?'

Hayley got it. 'You're an alien.'

'Yes.'

'And so am I.'

'Yes.'

Hayley laughed. 'Bullshit.'

Yeah. Total bullshit. What does this wanker take me for?

Alien?

'The minute I sniffed you, I realised. Jane was pregnant. She bore an egg inside her. You carry the aroma of it with you. That means –'

'Don't go there.'

'You have been fertilised.'

'Do NOT go there!' she said.

'But instead of embracing her, your own beloved mother, what did you do? You *smashed her face to pieces with a fire extinguisher*! I saw it! I saw what you did! You are a – *monster*!'

He was screaming. Spittle flecked his jaw, and sizzled on his skin. And as she stared at him, his face morphed.

Or rather, it changed its expression, terrifyingly. The calm pleasant look gave way to a mask of pure, primal hate.

'I didn't do –' 'Don't lie! I know what you did, you evil – evil –'

Franco spat at her; a thick gob of spittle that sprayed over her face, her eyebrows, her nose. No one had ever spat at her before; Hayley was stunned.

The spit dried on her. Like a face mask. It began to burn her skin.

'Yes, I know, I know exactly what you did, you evil bitch,' he told her.

'What are you talking about?' She was whimpering, her guilt carved on her heart.

Franco reached into his jacket pocket and took out a knife in a scabbard. 'Thirteenth century, her family heirloom,' he said. He slid the knife out of the leather scabbard. He showed her the blade. It was beautiful, half a foot long, curved, impossibly sharp. He touched the tip to her neck. She felt a trickle of blood. She didn't dare gulp.

Alone, in an empty room, in an empty corridor, with a lunatic who has a knife to my throat. Not good, Hayley, even by your standards.

'Don't deny it, creature,' Franco said. 'She told me everything, you see. You stabbed her, and stabbed her again. You stabbed her brain. You cut it to pieces. You smashed her head to pieces.. She was my wife, and I loved her. And she was one of your own kind, and she reached out, she begged you for friendship, and instead you killed her.'

He was weeping. The knife was trembling in his hand. Snot was dribbling out of his nose. He was battered with grief, and regret; and, Hayley suddenly realised, not dangerous at all. In fact she felt sorry for him.

'Put the knife down,' she said gently.

His puppy dog eyes stared back at her; his grief was almost touchable. 'Put the knife down.'

He put the knife down.

'Are you really what you say you are?' she asked.

He nodded, his beautiful face scarlet and blotchy, his cheeks and jaw damp with tears and phlegm. He was abject. Cowardice poured off him like sweat.

This *is the alien invasion?*

'I'm sorry for what I did,' Hayley said cautiously. 'But you see I was afraid. I thought she was going to kill me. I didn't know – it was – you have to – forgive me. Please. Will you do that?'

Franco paused a long while but could not deny her. He nodded.

'I forgive you,' he said. 'Because you are –'

'Don't say it,' said Hayley, finally putting the pieces together.

'– my –'

'Don't!'

'– daughter.'

That did it for Hayley. Her eyes erupted; her tears began to roll.

'This is Control to Echo Five, confirm position, Over,' said Marlowe, from his belvedere office in The Calls, not far from Leeds railway station.

'Approaching target destination now Control, Over.'

Marlowe could picture the scene: The Nighthawk jets swooping low over the rolling Yorkshire hills, flying below military radar, stealthed to be invisible as shadows on a dark and moonless night. If the planes were spotted there would be a cover story to justify their presence; but they were never spotted.

The Nighthawks took their aerial positions outside the town; they were the backstop, in case the hostiles made an attempt to flee by helicopter or car. Marlowe was taking no chances.

Within ten minutes of sending a mass mail-out of the photograph of Jane Carter's husband Billy Franco, at Marlowe's order, they'd got a positive ID – and, ironically, it came from a member of the surveillance team shadowing Hayley Bradley in Hebden Bridge. A waiter had been seen talking to Hayley, and he matched the photo and description. The agent had taken a picture and messaged it across. The ID was now confirmed by facial recognition software; it was Billy Franco.

There was as yet no intel about the presence or otherwise of an Exter nest in Hebden Bridge with access to escape vehicles, but Marlowe had learned the hard way to be cautious. Hence, the Nighthawks.

Marlowe was a man of firm and deeply-held principles. And in his view, Jane Carter had been a traitor to her kind. A betrayer of the sacred deal that he and Rothbury had negotiated all those years ago.

Carter had been selected – randomly and fairly – to be the yearly Andromeda for her region. Yet she had fled rather than allow herself to be righteously drained.

And the husband who had helped her escape was just as culpable, so Marlowe strongly believed. He had breached the accord that had preserved the peace between the two sentient species of Earth, the homeboys and the invaders, for so many centuries.

There is always an infidel.

And always must the infidel be slain.

In Hebden Bridge, vans from Leeds were arriving bearing ground troops. Twenty of them in all, clad in DOH camouflage uniform aka jeans and hoodies and brown and black face paint.

'This is Control to Echo Six, confirm position, Over,' said the voice of the DOH Commander over their radio channel; they all recognised it as Marlowe.

'Control this is Echo Six, just driving into Hebden Bridge now, Over.'

'Thank you, Echo Six, Out.

'Control to Echo Seven, confirm position, Over.'

'Parked up, Control, debarking now, Over.'

'Control to Echo Seven –'

'Where've you been?'

'I've been crying.'

Cheyney beamed. 'Because of me?'

Hayley stood, awkward in the long and lovely dress she didn't know how to wear, after half an hour of sobbing her eyes out.

'Yeah, sentimental, see.'
'Bless you.'
Cheyney opened up her arms: sisterly benediction.
'Don't hug me.'
'Hug.'
They hugged.

'And now the first number of the evening. The bride's choice, so let's see you on the dance floor, and let's have a round of applause for Cheyney and Liam.'

Cheyney's choice: Kings of Leon, Sex on Fire. The dance floor slowly filled. The dancing became a swarming. Fists began punching, crotches were grabbed. A raunchy crowd-pleaser, this one, and the crowd loved it.

'Yeah-hoh, your sex is on fire!' the wedding guests sang.

Hayley remembered Jane Carter's whispered words: 'Touch me.'

Hayley remembered: A hand outstretched, fingers splayed.

Hayley remembered: Jane Carter's pale face, expressionless, a blank mask that had tried to convey to her an emotion, but which emotion? *Friendship. Was she really offering me friendship?'*

A new song played: Guns N' Roses, Sweet Child of Mine.

Why did I do those terrible things to her? Was I really that afraid?

She remembered Franco's explanation of the history of his kind. 'Humans hate us. They hunt us. They torture us. They treat us worse than animals. All we want is to be left alone.'

The song played:
'Sweet child of mine
Sweet love of mine.'

The song ended. Now Ed Sheeran sang: 'Sing'.

'Dance?' She blinked, looked up. It was Liam.

'Nah, fuck off,' she advised him.

'Pity dance, that's all I'm offering.'

She tried not to smile but that didn't work.

'Go dance with your wife.'

'I've got my whole life ahead of me to dance with my wife. Tonight, I want to dance with my bloody sister in law. Come on, darling. Show me your moves.'

Hayley stared at him, inexpressibly touched.

Then she started weeping again. Tears poured down her cheeks. Liam was stunned.

He pulled her to her feet and gave her a hug. A big-brotherly hug. Over his shoulder Hayley could see Cheyney beaming at her; one big happy family, this was making her night.

'I know I know, you're happy for Cheyney.'

'I'm pregnant,' she snuffled.

'What!'

'No! No!' She'd got that SO wrong. 'I'm not pregnant, what I mean is, I've been fertilised by another woman's egg, so that makes me – makes me –'

'Drunk?' Liam hazarded.

She snuffled again, broke free.

'Are you on something, darling? Because if you are, that's fine by me. I just want to –'

She ran from him.

Pregnant? Don't be stupid, Hayley. I'm not pregnant. I'm as far from being pregnant as you can be. What I am is something different. What I am is –

I'm, yeah. I'm an – I'm – what I am is –

She couldn't bring herself to think the word.

I'm – different.

Even more different than I was before.

Alien. I'm an alien.

The roof terrace. Drunk, again. Alone, as always. The full moon was unblinking above the town of Hebden Bridge. The stars flickered like Christmas decorations, except they weren't. They were distant stars. Millions of them, tens of millions, hundreds of millions, a massive universe of stars up there. Suns and planets. And creatures living there too.

Hayley knew the theory. Granted the vast size of the universe and the durability of life, it was a miracle that not once, never, had a alien visitor come to this planet. So many stars, and none of them bore life?

Not so unlikely then, Franco's story. That a thousand years or so ago –

Ah, yes – Scorpions, Winds of Change. She could hear the music wafting out of the windows of the reception suite, into the night air.

'The future's in the air

I can feel it everywhere.'

The time has come for the midnight dance. The cake has been cut and the slices have been dispersed. Cake triangles sit on paper plates barely eaten. The tables are cluttered with empty glasses, slick pools of spilled beer shine under the ceiling globes. Pharrell Williams, happy as fuck, has been and gone and now John Legend sings of Ordinary People.

The dancers dance. Hayley, back in the Waterfront Hall, sits and watches.

I should join in. I should. Join in. I really should.

She doesn't. She sits. She watches.

Billy Franco was at her shoulder again.

'Can I walk you home?' he asks.

Her body language said no.

'Will you meet me tomorrow then?'

No.

'Can we talk?'

She shook her head.

'We have to talk.'

'No. No more talking. I never want to see you again. You or any of your –' She hissed the words: '– monstrous kind.'

'You're one of us now, Hayley. You –'

'Not possible. I have a Mam. I have a dad. Had.'

'One of us. Genetic material has been transmitted into you, through the hatching of –'

'Birds have eggs. I'm human.'

'Please, let me walk you home.'

She thought about it. Eventually, she nodded.

In the day time this is a quiet idyllic Yorkshire town.

But at night Hebden Bridge comes alive. Every pub is full. There are pissheads at the bar tanking it, oldtimers at their hallowed tables telling tall tales. Hikers sit in the snugs of old pubs, sipping real ale, aching from the day's punishing schedule.

Teenagers mill on the streets, blagging booze from off-licences. By the canal, wide-eyed tourists from America and Canada and the South of

England admire the history and quaintness of this quaint historic Northern town.

For local folk with aspirations, it's the perfect spot for a wedding.

Tonight the full moon has dark clouds framing it. Stars cluster in the sky – there's nowhere near the amount of light pollution you get in the city. And, invisible to the naked eye and to military radar, the Nighthawks hover like kestrels on an updraft, missiles primed; keeping Yorkshire safe for humankind.

On the ground the hit team have taken their positions. The two undercover agents continue to report on the progress of the wedding reception. One is pretending to be a cousin of one of the bridesmaids, the other is a waiter like Franco. Their whispered reports tell the squad that Hayley Bradford has exited the party and is lingering outside the Town Hall, in the company of an IC1 male who has been positively ID'd as Franco, William. She is TWP; he is to be taken alive.

Two birds, one stone. An exfiltration and a collateral damage.

The three commandments for this kind of operation are speed and containment and efficient disposal. There are two vans parked outside the town hall, to take the bodies away. And when the snatch takes place, a firework display will go off in the car park of the Shoulder of Mutton to create noise and distraction.

Marlowe is watching on a monitor in his office in the Calls. The window is open; he can feel the night air, and can hear the occasional night time revellers on their way to or from somewhere in Leeds. Once, he muses, he would have been out there, on the ground, with the hit squad. But he has managerial responsibilities now.

'This is Echo Three, Target sighted, all units take their positions, Over.'

'Roger that, Echo Three, all units proceed at your discretion, this is Control, signing Out.'

'It's cold.'

'You want my jacket?'

'Sokay, I don't really feel the cold.'

'Make your mind up.'

Hayley smiled. 'I mean, I do feel the cold but it doesn't bother me. It's the sun I hate. I peel if there's an advert for Majorca on the telly.'

'Where's your B&B?'

'This way.'

They walked away from the Town Hall, towards her B&B, enjoying the night. Franco didn't take her arm but he if he had, she woudn't have minded. She had forgotten, in all the flurry of the night, his earlier threat to murder her. She didn't even care, because she was very drunk, that he was technically her father. She felt strange in the long gown, not a bit like herself, but it was nice. They could see the canal now.

The path was suddenly very busy; a bunch of youths were blocking their way. And out of nowhere a policeman in uniform appeared, smiling. No, he was Community Liaison, not a real copper. 'Good evening, sir, madam. Are you with the wedding party?'

'Yes, we are.'

'We've had some trouble, you see. Some lads rucking. Best to go back, the other way.'

'Right, sure.'

'Evening, officer,' said Billy Franco.

'Right you are, lad.'

They turned, but as they did so some of the youths walked around them, then stopped, forming a semicircle, blocking the way.

Then the skies erupted in flame; a huge bang rocked the silence. Fireworks.

'That's nice, is that for Chey —'

The uniformed copper was holding a taser; he fired it at Hayley. She had a moment to glimpse what was happening, and then her body was convulsing.

She fell to her knees. She puked. She couldn't move, except for her rickety trembling. One of the youths moved forward and put handcuffs on her, very fast. She was vomiting, yet she was choked up too. Tears burned her eyes. She forced her head up and saw hazily that Franco had been tasered too, by a second uniformed copper. He was puking out a thin stream of vomit in front of him. Then the copper and two of the youths grabbed him and tried to cuff him.

Hayley's vision blurred again. Not the tears this time, it was just that Franco moved so quickly. He backpunched one of the youths and there was a crack like wood breaking. He picked up the other lad and threw him — literally threw him — across the pavement. The lad seemed to be suspended in air for an age. Then he crashed on to the hard cobbles and was still.

Another 'youth' who looked as if he was in his thirties stepped forward with a baton and smashed Franco in the mouth. Then again in the skull. Bones cracked. Hayley screamed — but a gag was being pulled over her mouth. The skies erupted again; a snowflake of light exploded and turned into a kaleidoscope of falling colours. A second huge firework rained purple light. A third huge firework came a second later; purple rain gave way to exploding red fireballs.

The sound was deafening; Hayley added it all up and got four. She tried to focus on her surroundings; she realised they had been cleverly bunched in on the narrow pathway, hidden from view of walkers in either direction. And as far as any passers-by were concerned, this was just a couple of coppers coping with a gang of angry drunks. Par for the course on a Saturday night in this part of Yorkshire.

'In the van with them,' said the Community Liaison copper, and then his face exploded. Hayley saw Franco take a step back – and realised he must have leaped five feet to punch the sergeant.

Hayley carried on thinking it through. These coppers weren't coppers, and the hoodies weren't hoodies either. This wasn't an arrest. She couldn't let herself –

Hayley spat out the gag. And she screamed.

Then she got to her feet and her eyes cleared, and she clapped her hands in front of her, so hard she felt the air flinch. She had been wearing handcuffs but now she wasn't; she must have broken them with her convulsive arm movement. She saw there was a snapped chain dangling from one wrist. One of the fake coppers swung a baton at her head and she dodged the blow and kicked his feet away from him, and stomped him, and his head burst, like a ripe fruit struck with a mallet. Franco stood beside her, shoulder to shoulder.

'Leave us al –' he said, then one of the youths shot him. It was an automatic pistol, firing a fast burst of bullets; Franco's body was punched with holes. But he was still standing. Another youth stood behind him, holding a strange device, a wire connected to two sticks; and he wrapped the wire around Franco's neck and pulled. At the same moment, he put his foot against Franco's back and kicked, convulsively. It was a savagely powerful move. In an instant the wire ripped through the neck and Franco's head was severed from its body and fell off, to bounce on the ground. His headless body slowly fell, spraying out arterial blood. Hayley whimpered.

A baton hit her on the head and she blacked out for an instant. Then she blinked and she was seeing stars and the man with the piano wire was behind her now, and the wire was biting into her throat. She felt an artery burst. Blood was gushing out. She was dying. It was all –

No I won't let you do this.

Hayley's body was vividly alive. She could feel the pain from the wire; she could hear her blood spurting out, she could sense her body rocking with the thump thump of her heart beat; and her arteries were roaring like cataracts tumbling off a cliff. And then her skin itched, and she realised her Celtic Cross tattoo on her arm was blazing hot, and she thought about the butterfly tattoo under her chin, her beautiful iridescent-blue Morpho butterfly from the Amazon, and she breathed the breath of her life into it.

The killer put his foot in Hayley's back and prepared to kick. He wasn't aware of the skin under her chin flapping and twisting. He didn't realise that the blue Morpho butterfly was shimmering like iron turning indigo in the heat of a forge. He wasn't conscious of the fact that the butterfly tattoo had detached itself from Hayley's flesh, ripping itself off; or that it flew up into the air faster than lightning and landed unerringly on his face.

All the killer knew is that one moment he was garrotting his hapless victim; the next, some flapping creature had ripped his eyeball out with sharp claws. He screamed and relaxed his grip. The two-dimensional blue butterfly flapped again and his other eyeball was pecked away. The assassin flailed his arms, like a scarecrow scaring off a parliament of crows, and stumbled backwards.

I'm alive.

Hayley was experiencing a weird time distortion; time was moving slowly, very slowly, which meant she was able to map the geometry of the scene in her head and consider her options. What next? Run? Fight? Save Franco?

She rolled forward, towards his body-less head, and she picked it up by the ponytail. The mouth was silently screaming, the eyes were blazing with rage – it was still alive! She saw filaments emerging and writhing from the neck stump, damp with blood, struggling to form into legs.

Hayley rolled the head towards the body, like a bowling ball aimed at skittles. Her aim was true. And in a trice, the legged head scuttled up on to the shoulders of the decapitated body; the filaments plunged into the twitching torso, growing into his flesh like roots in damp earth; and an instant later Franco was whole, and alive.

Then they all shot her.

There were a dozen or more of them still standing, a bizarre blend of coppers in uniforms and hoodies with stuck-on acne, all of them carrying handguns and they were shooting her. It was like being buffeted by a hurricane; she couldn't even feel the bullets, she just felt herself shaken and rocked and when a bullet went through her eye she thought that was it. She said her goodbyes, silently.

The shooting stopped. Hayley was a statue made of wounds, drenched in blood.

'No more,' said a gasping voice. 'No more.'

It was Franco. Standing upright. Like Hayley, he was a scarlet tower; he should have been dead, he absolutely should have been dead. But life persisted in him. It was there in his eyes, his hate-filled eyes.

And the blood on the cobbled ground all around him began to sizzle.

And the blood on his skin steamed and sizzled too, like scarlet sweat.

And the sizzling blood on the ground and on his skin sprang into the air and it coalesced into a cloud, and it billowed out as red mist, as if Franco were a wizard surrounded by demonic fog. And his eyes were still full of hate and weeping blood; and that blood too was alive and angry. And when he moved his hand, the blood compressed, and formed into tiny capsules that hovered like tiny bombers. Compacted tiny blood corpuscles with the density of steel.

Hayley saw, and understood. And her own blood was around her too, a protecting cloak that at the beckon of her will coalesced and turned into dark scarlet bullets.

She thought her thought; Franco thought his thought too, at exactly the same instant.

And the blood bullets fired.

Another snowdrop of light exploded in the sky but by now the game was up; two dozen phone calls had been made to the police reporting gunfire.

Meanwhile, the cobbled ground around the canal was awash with blood; the bodies of the fake coppers and the fake hoodies were strewn this way and that, faces frozen in shock, bodies butchered and rent by supersonic bullets of blood.

It was as if the hand of God had smote them all, all these sinners and murderers with their fake coloration and phoney accents; miraculously transforming a cabal of cold-eyed killers into dead flies, crushed, by wanton boys.

And Franco and Hayley were gone.

The waters of the Rochdale Canal shuddered as the movement of their bodies created ripples that lapped the stone embankment.

Above those trembling waters a tiny creature hovered, an impossible being of iridescent blue with powerful wings, a butterfly that could see and hear and fly but had no organs, no brain, no depth.

Below it, the waters of the Rochdale Canal turned dully red under the sheen of street lights as Hayley and Franco swam to freedom.

They swam for two hours bumping along the canal bed, with no need to breathe, and as they swam their wounds slowly healed. Bullet wounds in their skulls and torsos and limbs, cracked bones, ripped flesh, even Hayley's long-dead eyeball. All were healed as the two sentient swarms of microparasites from an alien planet regenerated their human host organisms.

As they swam, hugging the canal's muddy breast, frog-kicking at a pace that would have put to shame an Olympic champion, the infected bodies spat out bullets and left a train of spent metal slugs nearly six miles long.

Eventually, far outside the town, among the rolling hills of West Yorkshire, the two wedding guests clambered sodden out of the bloodied canal and crashed on to the tow path. They were on open land now, far from any houses or roads. The butterfly had recced the scene shrewdly for them, guided by Hayley's controlling mind.

Hayley was in the air, darting on updrafts, peering all around; and also she was on the ground, flat on her back, breathing heavily, in, out, in, out. Wondering why she was panting so much when she no longer needed to breathe.

The butterfly flickered downwards and landed on her face, tickling her with its blue wings. It hopped on to her chin, down on to her neck. Then it joined her body again: to become a blue butterfly tattoo inscribed on the skin between her throat and her jaw. Its mind merged with her mind; she was one again.

And a moment later she cut loose from the blood trails that she'd left behind in the canal, and felt a wrench. It was a strange sensation, like losing a layer of skin. Hayley felt giddy as her thousands of selves collapsed into a unitary intelligence.

Franco was beside her, motionless.

They lay there until dawn and then they got up.

Four

Hayley watched Liam for a long while, wary of committing herself.

He was alone, as she had insisted. Sitting at a table for two with his back to a pillar. A big man, at ease with himself, nursing a pint of bitter. Alert, aware of his surroundings, like an animal in the jungle.

Just as Hayley was. Her flesh tingled. She could smell lager and beer and pale ale and whisky and gin and Jägerbombs and slices of lime. Sweaty bodies. Eau de cologne and perfume and old socks and cotton. It was intoxicating. She damped it all down, till all she had was vision and hearing. Then she got up and strode forward. Showtime.

'Hey,' said Hayley, and sat down at the beer-damp table. Liam nodded calmly, as if she'd arrived dead on time to a schedule set by him.

'The prodigal, eh?'

She'd been missing for a month and then she'd called Liam out of the blue and here she was again. On the cadge, once more. Looking to get hold of some of his 'fucking money' so she could live a life on the run with her father from another planet.

Ah Hayley you are a piece of work, Hayley thought.

For the first two weeks after the massacre, Hayley and Billy had lived in the mountains around Hebden Bridge, until the search parties had given up. Living on no food and no water, drenched by the rain, sleeping without shelter on bitterly cold nights in the Yorkshire wilds. For Hayley it was the happiest time of her entire life

Since the events at Hebden Bridge, every part of her body was *alive*. Her skin her eyes and ears her teeth her fingernails and, most of all, now you come to mention it, her *skin*. All of it from the skin on her nose to the skin on the backs of her toes. When it rained, she could feel each drop of water. When she was cold she could feel the chatter of her teeth like an orchestra in her head.

It was like being blind and deaf and colour blind and semi-comatose and then – suddenly and instantly – becoming healed and getting all those sensations back in a thunderflash.

Billy however was in a bad way. His physical injuries had finally healed, though more slowly than hers. But psychologically he had been damaged by the events that night at Hebden Bridge. They had defied their enemies and they had killed many of them – probably all of them. And Hayley was fine with that. All she had done was defend herself. It was her or them, and, frankly, she was delighted that it was them.

But Billy felt *guilty*. He had broken the rules of his kind. He had stood and fought and that, so he firmly believed, was a sin in the eyes of a God who, justifiably, now despised him. And so Billy was lost in sadness and depression and, let's face it, self-pity. He was both wretched and pathetic, and Hayley was sorely tempted to abandon him.

Eventually she had to leave him in a state of stupor in the hills while she went foraging. She memorised the landmarks, piled bracken on his motionless body, then she had travelled down into the valley at the dead of night until she spotted a five star hotel.

She snuck into the grounds and broke in via a back door with the intention of stealing clothes and money from one of the rooms. Her wedding gown had pretty much fallen off her after she had crawled out of the canal; stiff with blood, drenched, and riddled with bullet holes. And her shoes were worse than useless.

And so she travelled naked and barefoot from her refuge in the mountains into the hotel. She could move so silently that only an owl could hear her tread. She did not breathe. The only noise she made was when she slammed the door of one of the rooms with her palm to break the lock; and then she was inside. And though it was pitch black she could see everything.

That night, she stole a tweed suit and brogues for Billy, a top and skirt and sensible shoes for herself, several jackets, and a wallet and purse with about three hundred pounds cash inside. The shoes were too big but the rest looked fine.

Then she unerringly made her way back up the mountain and found Billy dead. His heart had stopped. She guessed he had made it stop. He did not breathe; she assumed he had chosen to stop breathing.

She watched him for a while and wept. And after she had wept a long while, she touched the tears with the tips of her fingers, and placed her finger tips upon his eyelids.

The salty moisture oozed off the skin of her fingers and entered his eyes; and made his tear ducts spill forth their juices.

Thus, her tears mingled with *his* tears; and through this sentient commingled moisture she silently spoke to him: *'Get a bloody grip, Billy. And that's an order.'*

Billy snapped out of his coma.

'What have you done to me?' Billy whined out loud.

Hayley stroked his forehead, the poor sad boy.

'We won, Billy. They lost. Is that so bad?' she said to him.

'I am a traitor to my –'

She raised a finger to hush him.

Her tears spoke softly: *'You are a hero. You saved my life. If it wasn't for you, I would be dead. Billy! Take pride in what you did. You saved my life. Jane – your beloved Jane would be proud of you.'*

That did it.

Then his tears spoke back to *her* tears, begging forgiveness.

And Billy was back.

After which, the two of them had returned to civilisation. But Hayley was tired of stealing clothes and food and other people's purses. Hence, Liam.

'Sorry I, you know,' said Hayley. She had no idea what precisely she was apologising for.

'We thought you were dead,' Liam said calmly.

'I almost was.'

Liam was glancing around. Looking for what? Undercover cops? An escape route?

'So what happened?' he asked. 'You didn't stay in your B&B that night. The night of the wedding, I mean. You weren't there when we got back from honeymoon. Chey was – fair play, that was out of order, girl.'

'There was an explosion.'

'Yeah, I know. Gas main. Two people died.'

'More than two.'

'You saw it?'

'I *was* it. Long story. Liam, I'm in trouble.'

Liam stopped glancing around and stared at her for a long time. His hard man stare. Testing her, she guessed.

They were in a Bradford 'spoons, the Titus Salt it was called. A vast palace of booze on several floors. Hayley had medium-length brown hair now, she'd lost the tunnel piercings and the tattoos; she was wearing a Monsoon dress. It had taken Liam a moment or so to even recognise her.

'What kind of trouble?' he said eventually.

'With the law.'

'Ah, then you've come to the right man.'

'And the government.'

'You're losing me now.'

'I'm being hunted by a secret society called the Defenders of Humanity.'

He flinched. 'And now I'm going to pretend I've never seen you before.'

'They tried to kill me, Liam.'

'Your sister,' Liam said pointedly. 'Cried her fucking eyes out. On our honeymoon. Her Mam was texting her five times a day, she was worried sick.'

'I seriously doubt that.'

'That your Mam cares about you?'

'She doesn't give a shit about anyone, let alone me.'

Liam was rarely exasperated but now he was: 'What is it with you, Hayley? How come you are always the bloody victim? Always the one who's hard done by, what's that about, hey?'

Hayley thought about the thirteen years, from the time she was four to the time she was seventeen, when every day her mother would shout at her or hit her or poke her with pins. The pins were a masterstroke because you could never see the marks. And all the while, Cheyney was the best girl, the favourite girl, the princess.

'I guess I'm a spoiled brat,' she conceded.

'Well,' said Liam.

'I was always jealous of Chey,' Hayley admitted. 'She was the pretty one. I was the – I don't know what I was.'

'You're pretty.'

'Don't tell me I'm fucking pretty, you dick! I will not be defined by how pretty I am or am not!'

'You scrub up well, too, glad you got rid of those piercings.'

'Damn you Liam, I will not be defined by how I look!'

'My point is, a lot of boys – or girls come to that – who might otherwise find you attractive might well be discouraged by the fact you're angry all the time and you dress like you are the potatoes in a sack.'

She had to smile at that one.

'I need money, Liam.'

That was hardly news to him.

'How serious is this, exactly?'

'They tried to kill me. People are trying to kill me.'

He was giving her a sad look.

'I'm not making this up. I'm not delusional.'

'Who is trying to kill you? This secret society?' Liam scoffed.

Hayley took out the serrated camping knife she had bought in the sporting goods shop; and she cut off her little finger with a single fast jerk.

Blood spurted.

She made a gobbet of her blood leap into the air and spell Liam's name above the table. Then she made her severed little finger dance. Meanwhile, she healed the stump so it stopped spurting.

Liam absorbed all this. In fairness, he gave good deadpan.

'Will that grow back, like?'

'Of course.'

'Then what happens to –'

'It'll – well I don't know.' Hayley had never cut off a finger before. She had no idea if it would shrivel and die or live a whole separate live as a semi-sentient autonomous finger.

She wrapped the finger in a food napkin and slipped it in her purse.

'Money, Liam. And somewhere to live. Please?'

Liam was considering all the options; you could almost see the cogs whirr. 'What are you, Hayley?'

'Hard to say.'

He drained his pint. He stared into space. 'What do I tell your sister?'

'Tell her I'm okay. No, tell her nothing. No –'

'I'll tell her you're a raving lunatic and you've run away to Spain.'

'She knows I'm a lunatic. Why Spain?'

'Jesus, Hayley. I need another drink.'

'I'll get one in.'

She waited.

'But can I have some money first?'

'I do so enjoy our little chats,' Gwendolyn said amiably.

'The pleasure is entirely – not mutual,' said Jane Carter.

Jane tried to smile but she no longer had functioning muscles in her face. She had not seen herself in a mirror since that day when the purple-haired woman had smashed her skull into pieces. But she guessed that she was a piece of work. Her skull had healed together, the brain she had left had reconnected with her neurological system, and most importantly her blood now pumped freely around the husk of flesh that was all she could call a body. But she was not human, by any stretch of the imagination. She was an organism with a human mind and an alien intellect and a body that had knitted together as randomly as a forest of weeds.

And here she was, chained to a wall in Rothbury's castle. A dismal life some might say and yet she was content.

Jane felt kinship with Lady Gwendolyn. They were of the same social class – aristocrats through and through. They were both born as only daughters in families full of strong-willed men who were barons and earls and knights and they both knew what it was to have to fight to be your own woman.

'The gardens are looking glorious,' Gwendolyn said. 'I wish you could see them. The Rhododendron Dell. The cherry blossoms.'

'Sounds lovely.'

The dungeon was brighter now. At Gwendolyn's insistence, electric lights had been installed. Tapestries were draped on walls, the ones from the east wing. There was a music player so that the prisoners could listen to Bach and Ravel and Mozart and, at Jane's request, Elvis Presley and Billy Fury. They were still prisoners, they were still chained, but at least they had some creature comforts now.

'What else?' Gwendolyn prompted.

'All I know is that we came from a larger planet than this and we lived in three different kinds of sentient life forms. But it was the scaly three legged ones that built us the ships that travelled through space.'

'So you have already told me,' Gwendolyn said reprovingly.

'Because that is all I know.'

'But where did you land? And why did your host bodies die? They must have had space suits. They must have had weapons. Why didn't they conquer the Earth? Back then, you would not have had much to contend with.'

Gwendolyn was writing a history of the Exters. It was hard, though, for Exters have no concept of history. They have attributes and intelligence but no self-consciousness. They have survival instincts but no strategy for survival. Try asking Julius Caeser's flu virus for a history of the decline and fall of the Roman Empire; that was the challenge Gwendolyn had set herself.

'I do not know.'

'I asked you to think about it. Did you think about it?'

'Yes.'

'And?'

'I still do not know.'

Were her people really from an alien planet? Jane didn't even know that much for sure. All she knew was that there was an immortal part of her. A part that controlled her by forcing her to be cowardly, and venal, and selfish. For centuries she had thought that was her actual personality. But now she knew better. The parasite-mind was in her, part of her, nestled up against her Jane-mind. Making her the worst possible version of herself. But it was not *her.*

She could see it in Billy too. She'd always loved him but at times he had shocked her with his shallowness and gutlessness. He shirked confrontation. He stole what he could easily have earned. He did not share. When times were hard he ran away instead of standing his ground. He would never, in any circumstances, fight for what he believed in. But that wasn't Billy. That was parasite-mind-Billy. The real Billy was noble, and good. So Jane believed.

'And tell me again how you escaped?' asked Gwendolyn.

'I cannot remember,' Jean said.

'You must remember. It was barely nine months ago.'

'Perhaps my chains broke.'

'You must have broken them.'

'They are unbreakable.'

'Then how did they break?'

'I can't remember.'

Jane remembered well. Her Defender escort picked her up from their flat in Liverpool to take her to her destiny. She was loaded up in the back of a furniture van with a dozen or so other Andromedas. Before she left, Billy had kissed her goodbye. But once the van pulled off she broke her chains with a single twist of her wrists and broke the doors with a kick and jumped off into the road. Then she sprinted back to Billy. The van drove on and her absence wasn't noticed for some time. The other prisoners, even though she had released them, refused to follow her.

After persuading Billy to run away with her, which took some time, Jane had stolen a car and driven them north to Bradford. There they lived for a few glorious weeks, while her baby grew in her brain. But then they were spotted and had to flee again. This time, she was caught.

'More to the point, why did you escape?'

'Wouldn't you?' Jane asked.

Gwendolyn's eyes darted around at the emaciated prisoners in chains hanging from walls. All of them, including Jane, were desperately weak from blood loss – no breaking chains *here*. None of them had sanitary facilities. The smell was vile, even though they were squirted with soap and hosed down twice a day.

'But you had a reason, didn't you?' Gwendolyn asked.

Jane said nothing.

Gwendolyn looked sad. Jane knew she was feeling guilty.

Even so, she looked terrific. Gwendolyn's hair was still grey and her face was still wrinkled. But there was a spring in her step, and a zest in her bearing. The terrible scar-like wrinkles on her brow had faded and she now looked characterful and mature, rather than a wizened crone. Her eyes were no longer rheumy. Her hearing was acute. She bore herself like an active sixty-year-old, not an arthritic eighty-year-old. She was getting younger by the day.

But there was a price to pay. Guilt was her price.

Hence, the tapestries and the Bach.

'Do you ever wish you could have children, Jane?' Gwendolyn asked.

With no functioning muscles in her face, Jane did not have to strive to remain deadpan. Yet she felt her heart skip a beat.

'Of course not. To bring a child into this life would be a crime.'

'That means you do miss having children. I do, you know. Hugh and I, we never – but there you go.'

'If I had a child, I would call it Gwendolyn,' Jane said.

'Oh now you're buttering me up.'

'I'm glad you come and talk to me. These are the best moments of my day,' Jane lied.

Somewhere out there, Jane's child lived. Her Exter-child, her parasite-brain child was alive in the body of that purple-haired girl. An unthinking unfeeling uncaring alien entity but still *her* child.

That gave her solace.

'I know all about it,' said Gwendolyn. 'Hugh explained it in terrible detail. For one of your kind to be born, you must kill a baby. A human baby.'

'That's not how it works.'

'You are child killers.'

'No child ever dies.'

'But you possess its body and destroy its mind. That's the same as killing it.'

'Not so. I am still me,' said Jane. 'Someone, somewhere, hatched an egg in the vicinity of my baby self and that's how I have these powers. But I'm still me. I'm still human. Don't believe the lies these people tell. We do not kill babies. We *improve* babies.'

'Babykillers,' muttered Gwendolyn absently. 'Monsters, all of you.'

Clearly that thought gave her some comfort.

'It's full,' Jane said.

Gwendolyn closed the catheter on Jane's arm. She sealed the vial of fresh blood and labelled it with today's date. Then she reconnected Jane to a new bottle.

'You should drink it fresh,' Jane said slyly. 'It's nicer that way.'

'Dangerous,' Gwendolyn reproved. 'Blood has to age.'

'More exciting,' Jane goaded. 'Your husband likes it fresh. Sometimes he stabs my breasts and drinks from me as if he was my baby.'

'Don't be preposterous.'

'It's an aphrodisiac,' Jane explained. 'Did you not know? The men go crazy for it. Old blood makes you live forever. But new blood, that's a different kind of buzz entirely.'

Gwendolyn was frozen with disbelief.

'Don't lie to me, child,' said Gwendolyn in her haughtiest tones..

'There's still juice in this flesh,' Jane Carter told her, as she hung from dislocated arms, her skeleton-thin body pale, her skin wafery, her eyes glaring out of deep sockets from a face that bore no expression. 'Or so your husband tells me.'

'What kind of eggs?' Hayley asked.

'Scrambled.'

'How many?'

'Three.'

'How many sausages?'

'Oh, um. Two. No three.'

'You can have four.'

'Four then.'

'Bacon?'

'Yes.'

'Hash browns, and how many?'

'Yes and two.'

'Tomatoes and beans?'

'Yes.'

'Black pudding?'

'No.'

Hayley wrote the order down in her notepad, because she knew it annoyed people that she was able to memorise her orders so effortlessly.

She walked back to the counter and shouted: 'English breakfast three eggs scrambled four sausages two hash browns tomatoes beans no black pudding,' then ripped the order off the page and handed it to Lily to give to the chef. Mama Jones handed her a mug of tea from the infinity teapot on the stove, the one that got topped up all day long, seemingly without Mama ever changing the tea leaves.

'Thanks, Mama.'

'Good girl, Mary.'

Hayley took the tea to the customer. She took note of the four workmen in hi-vis vests who she guessed were digging up the road down the street. Two students earnestly discoursing, nursing hangovers. A couple of off duty coppers who never paid for their breakfasts even though that was strictly against regs these days. A guy with wire framed glasses who looked as if he'd meant to go in Costa's but couldn't find it.

'You ready to order?' she asked the students.

'Bacon sandwich for me. And a tea.'

'Tea and a tofu salad.'

'We don't do tofu.'

'Do you do salad?'

'We do bacon sandwich sausage sandwich coronation chicken sandwich barbecue chicken sandwich plain chicken sandwich full English Breakfast or Jamaican patties and everything else on the board. We do not do tofu.'

'No need to get shirty.'

'I wasn't getting shirty,' said Hayley, shirtily.

Mama ambled up. 'You want a salad? We can do a salad. What's tofu?'

'It's a kind of –'

'I know what it is.' Mama laughed. It was a deep laugh, as if a man were hiding in the recesses of her large body. 'Never tell the customer no, my lovely. We got all the –'

The door opened and trouble walked in. Two men and a woman in suits and Border Patrol orange vests.

'Take a seat gentlemen, madam,' Mama boomed.

'Are you Myfanwy Jones?' the sandy-haired one asked.

'I am,' said Mama proudly. It was a name she had adopted after hearing the song, even though she was born in the Caribbean and christened 'Belinda'.

'We need to interview all your staff, and we need four forms of ID and we will be doing biometric tests, as per the –'

'We're busy now, come back another day.'

'We have authorisation –'
'All right all right. All me staff are busy. Are you busy, Mary?'
'I was just about to clock off,' Hayley said and Mama's eyes narrowed.
'Off you go then.'
'You need to do a biometric –'
'Yes but I have a hospital –'
'No one leaves, 'the man said firmly. 'Those are the rules.'
Hayley shrugged.
'Four forms of identification? I don't have four forms of identification.'
'You have three days to produce –'
'Ah, such foolishness,' said Mama. For the first time since Hayley had known her, she saw Mama's spirit ebb. All these years living in a wet and irritable land, serving teas and cooked breakfasts for generation upon generation of South Londoners – and *this* was her reward?
'You first,' the man said to Hayley. A fingerprint box was produced and placed on a table. The cafe became a border control station. Hayley felt weary. This wasn't right.
'I need to go to the loo,' she said sweetly.
'Now!'
'I'm bursting.'
'Don't think you can run out the back way. ID, then fingerprints, then retinal –'
Hayley spat at him. The spit caught him smack in the face and spread over his skin like ice on glass. Then it boiled. He was stunned for a moment then he screamed. Steam billowed from his face. Hayley let the saliva cool and fall away. She didn't want to *hurt* him.
Hayley jumped up on a table with one leap. She bounced from table to table, avoiding the plates and the tea mugs, then threw herself through the window. She gave herself a big kick off the final table to speed up her flight, but even so it was touch and go – for a moment she was afraid she would bounce off the glass like a cartoon cat.
But instead she flew right through, head first. She landed on the pavement outside in a flurry of blood and broken glass. Her face was bleeding profusely. Her arm was broken. She stood up and saw a second Border Patrol team in a parked car. She ran away, very fast.
That night she and Billy left London and began a long walk along country paths, travelling only at night. Hayley's broken arm healed on the way. She never saw Mama again and never found out what happened to her.

It's like watching a dog trying to play the piano.

Bug bug bug bug bug bug bug bug!

God is Love. The Lord Thy God is Human. Thou shalt worship the Lord Thy God with every atom of thy being, but do not think thou hast a soul, for thou art naught but wicked vermin.

Servants serve, never forget that. You are a servant.

You think you are my friend! Don't make me laugh. Can a toenail be a friend?

Just do what I tell you and don't try and be clever. You cannot be clever, you stupid fucking virus.

Harry Barraclough had always been a timid man. His wife used to josh him about how shy he was. She used to boss him about, then tell him off for being so easily bossed about. Lots of Yorkshire men are like that, they're braggarts in the pub and poodles in their own home. And Harry does in fact believe that God is Love and that God is Human. And he accepts his place in the great Chain of Being, somewhere very near the bottom.

But this bastard Smith is really getting to him. He's the nastiest kind of public school git. Barraclough knows that Smith is older than he looks. But Smith *looks* young. He looks like a child. And to be constantly bossed about by a cheeky young nipper is more than Harry Barraclough can bear.

Yet bear it he must.

Marlowe was briefing the team. Smith, Henson, Brady, Evans, McGregor and Lloyd. Lloyd was the only human woman in the room. Barraclough and Jeanie Millican were the only Exters.

'I thank you for your diligence. We may not approve of this new strategy but we have executed it to the best of our ability, and the wrath of God has descended upon Yorkshire,' said Marlowe.

All the licensed nests were being closed down and the residents were being housed in secure units. Jails, in effect. Those with protected jobs were being allowed to go to work but now had to wear electronic tags. Barraclough and Millican both had tags around their ankles, drilled in to the bone so they could not be removed.

These were dark days for anyone who believed that Exters had a right to live in freedom and safety. But, or so it seemed, no one did.

'There has,' said Marlowe, 'been little or no resistance, as we expected. But there are murmurings.'

Barraclough knew of the murmurings. He said nothing.

'There is talk that Billy Franco is a saviour, and his name has become a rallying point.'

Barraclough knew this too. He said nothing.

'He must be found. DS Smith?'

'We believe Franco is with the woman, Hayley Bradley. We also believe that Hayley is in regular touch with her sister, Cheyney, perhaps by burner phone. So far we have not been able to intercept any messages.'

'Then do what you must,' said Marlowe.

That was how Barraclough and Smith came to be parked up outside Cheyney's new home. A big house in North Leeds, her husband was worth a bob or two. Surveillance teams ascertained that he had just left for work, which usually meant the pub. So Smith and Barraclough moved in. They went for the direct approach; they rang the front door bell.

'DS Smith, DC Barraclough,' said Barraclough, showing his warrant card. 'Can we come in, Miss?'

'What's it about?'

'We have news about Hayley,' lied Barraclough.

Her face lit up. She was a pretty young woman. Barraclough had a bad feeling about this.

'Let us in please, madam,' Smith said brusquely, and she opened the door and in they trod.

Paintings on the wall. Impressionist and Expressionist. Was that a Munch? Barraclough liked paintings. He went to galleries sometimes.

'Do you know where she is?' Cheyney asked.

'No but we've heard she's been recruited by Isis,' said Smith brutally.

Cheyney stared. 'Don't be absurd.'

'I'm serious. She's been radicalised.'

'Bullshit!'

'How do you know that?'

'Well she would have – she's not the type.'

'She would have what? Said something, last time you spoke to her?'

'I haven't – not since Hebden Bridge.'

She was breathless. Defensive. That was the Smith effect for you.

'That wasn't a gas mains explosion, it was a bomb. A terror bomb,' said Smith. 'Your sister is a terrorist. How does she speak to you? Do you use burner phones? How does she know the number?'

'I'm saying nowt,' said Cheyney, determined.

Smith punched her. It was a powerful blow and Cheyney fell and when she got up her nose was bloodied. But she was a fiery young woman and she faced Smith down.

'You're not fucking police at all, are you?'

'We are, in fact.' Smith smiled. 'That's the worrying thing, really, isn't it?'

'Get out!'

'Not until you give us the phone you used when you last spoke to your sister. You must have just the one burner. Hard enough to get one number to her, you can't keep changing phones. Where is it? It's not in your house.'

A covert team had searched the house from top to bottom when Cheyney was at the dentist's.

'So where then?'

'Do you know who my husband is? Do you know what he'll do to you?' Cheyney said spitefully.

'Your husband is a criminal, do as we say or we'll put him away for life,' said Smith.

'Go screw yourself.'

Smith smiled.

He truly was an unpleasant shit, Barraclough mused.

'DC Barraclough, you know what you have to do.'

'Yes sir. What, sir?'

'Force a confession, of course.'

'Yes sir.'

'Rape her first, maybe?'

Cheyney flinched. She looked confused. He couldn't be serious?

'Yes sir.' Barraclough took his jacket off.

God is Love.

Shit! He bloody means, it, thought Cheyney.

'You can't be – what the fuck –!' she said.

'Hurt her as much as you like. Humiliated women find it hard to stand mute, in my experience,' said Smith, briskly.

And what experience is that, sir? thought Barraclough.

God is Human and we are vermin.

You are daft as a brush, Harry Barraclough, but I never regret the day I married you.

You should stand up for yourself more! Have some bloody backbone. Ah you bloody fool, Harry Barraclough!

God is Love. And it is our duty to serve Him.

'Get on with it,' snapped Smith.

'You dare – you touch me – I'll fucking –' Cheney squared up, fists raised. Barraclough guessed she had some martial arts training from her stance.

'She's a bit feisty, sir, I thought I'd taser her first.'

'As you wish.'

Barraclough took out his taser. It was better than police issue, it fired five electrodes at once and delivered a dangerously powerful electric charge.

Barraclough tasered Smith.

It was point blank range, all five electrodes engaged and Smith fell like a stunned cow. His body shuddered and puke spilled out of his mouth. Barraclough looked at Cheyney and –

And Smith recovered with astonishing speed and lunged to his feet and elbow-struck Barraclough, making him drop the taser. Then, before Barraclough could pause for breath, Smith took his baton out and shook it and a long blade emerged. He stabbed at Barrarclough.

Barraclough dodged with dazzling speed but the blade slashed his face and arms and gouts of blood flew into the air.

Remember Hebden Bridge.

Smith struck at Barraclough's throat and Barraclough ducked and spun and was behind him.

Remember Hebden Bridge.

Barraclough took out his own crossed-bar baton but Smith spun around and head butted him and buried the blade of his knife-baton in Barraclough's throat. An artery was burst and a spray of blood reddened the air.

Remember Hebden Bridge.

Barraclough had been astonished when he surveyed the scene, as part of the clean-up team. It had been a massacre. Warriors in full body armour had been gunned down with invisible missiles. No one could explain what had happened. Exters are not violent, they have no natural weapons, and they are afraid to use guns. Billy Franco should not have been able to fight back and he should not have been able to kill all those people.

Now, fighting for his life, Barraclough's mind was racing and that made time slow down. He saw the cloud of blood from his burst artery in mid-air and realised that for the next few moments it was still his blood, his flesh. So he connected with it, he felt it. He controlled it.

He made the blood swarm like bees and then made the swarm fly across the room and then made it land on Smith's face like a mask. And then Barraclough made his own blood *boil.*

Smith's screams were stifled by the mask of blood that bubbled upon his face. He fell to his knees. The bubbling blood was mashed up now with his own blood and skin.

Barraclough reached out a hand to Cheyney. She stared blankly. 'We have to go,' he said, calmly.

Smith was still screaming. Barraclough guessed he was blind by this point. The blood continued to boil away until Barraclough was out of the front door, then suddenly he lost contact with it. But the damage was done.

Barraclough took out his keys and nodded at the CID car. 'Hop in,' he said.

'Jesus,' said Cheyney.

'We have to run. We need somewhere to hide. Will Liam help us?'

'Jesus! What the hell *are* you?'

'Alien.'

She took a moment, but no more than that. 'Okay.'

'Liam?'

Cheyney nodded, still dazed.

'Get in,' said Barraclough gently.

God is Love.

From Brixton, Hayley and Billy fled south to Hastings. They checked into a B&B, paying cash for everything. Behaving like illicit lovers, with lots of giggling and holding hands, to explain their refusal to use a bank card. Hayley had bought a laptop with Liam's money and they used Google to track strange events across the nation.

Billy had access to a darknet address where Exters posted gossip and news and this site had a new feature called YOU ARE NOT ALONE. There they found information about Exter nests disrupted or destroyed, couched in the coyest language.

Our friends in Roath in Cardiff have itchy feet and are no longer at that address. Our blessings go with them. Remember, God is Love.

The 'God is Love' mantra was part of the Exter brainwashing, Hayley had discovered. Billy was not religious but even he became docile and brainless when he heard the words God is Love.

Billy and Hayley had quarrelled often about this. 'You people choose to enslave yourselves. There are more of you than them! Fight back! Or at least, run away!'

'We cannot fight back. We cannot run away.'

'You did.'

'Jane did. She was not like others of our kind.'

No, Hayley realised – because she was *pregnant.*

'You fought at Hebden Bridge.'

Billy shook his head. Baffled at his own rage that night.

'Never before have I killed humans. Never before have I –'

'You did it for me. To save *me.*'

Yes, he did.

A father's love. More powerful, it seems, than God is Love.

They walked along the seafront most days. They ate in seaside cafes. They had fish and chips every lunchtime. Hayley discovered she could drink a bottle of wine at a sitting without getting remotely drunk and Billy told her she would never get cirrhosis. But there is only so much booze you can drink in a day.

Remember Hebden Bridge.

Every day, she thought about what had happened that night. She'd killed and fled and now she would never see her family again.

She spoke to Cheyney regularly on the phone number Liam had given her. It was for a 'burner' phone, he had said. The two sisters talked about everything except Hebden Bridge, and fish and chips. Because Hayley didn't dare leave any clues about where she was.

One day, Cheyney didn't answer. That was the day her sister had to leave behind the burner phone that she'd hidden under the marble kitchen floor of Liam's house; the day when she and Barraclough ran away from the blinded Detective Sergeant Smith.

Now Hayley felt truly alone.

YOU ARE NOT ALONE.

Exters were dying all across the country, and in Europe and America and Russia and China too. It was a genocide. Every day the darknet site carried more condolences:

We shall miss our friends from Peterborough. Eleven gallant comrades, now staying in gated accommodation somewhere – alas! – but we have no forwarding address.

Rest in Peace our friends from Bath. Twenty-four of them, they found they were no longer welcome in God's own country. For God is Love but not all guests are welcome it seems.

And then:

News from friends who are staying at the pleasure of our Christian Brothers. We are told that in Scotland in the lovely castle of Rothbury a new guest has arrived, one we feared was no longer with us, and her name is Jane Allison Carter. Greetings to you Jane, though we fear you may not be able to read this.

Hayley stared at the words. Impossible! It was completely impossible!

'Help me. Save me.'

Hands outstretched.

'We have to rescue her,' said Billy.

Hayley was torn between shock and relief and some other emotion she couldn't even identify.

'It's no kind of life. They will leech blood from her every day. She should not have to endure that.'

She cannot be alive. Not after what –

How could anything survive the injuries Hayley had inflicted?

'Please! We have to rescue –'

Billy had a crazed look in his eyes.

Discretion is.

'We can't, Billy,' Hayley said gently.

The better part.

'There are just two of us. You've told me how powerful these people are.'

'Yes, they are very powerful.'

'They are many we are few.'

'Yes.'

'So it's impossible. Even to try would be –'

Of valour. Who said that?

'I'll go on my own,' said Billy in a cracked voice.

She remembered what a coward he was.

She realised what a coward *she* was.

'We stand no chance,' she said firmly.

'You may be right but we have to try.'

She didn't recognise him, this man who stood before her now. Quietly resolute. Utterly determined. Blindly adoring of his soul mate, the woman who he had shared more than ten lifetimes with. Would anyone ever love *her* this much?

Hands outstretched. 'Help me. I'm begging you. Help!'

Hayley dug in. She gave Billy her angry look. She knew how easy it was to intimidate him. He was the kind of beta male who looked tearful if she told him he'd put too much sugar in her tea. 'You have to face facts,' she said sternly. 'It's too late to help her. She's gone. Lost to you. Oh grow up, Billy! You're not cut out to be a bloody hero. Nor am I! Just – let it go.'

'She is your mother,' Billy reminded her.

God is Love.

Hayley wept.

'Can I help you?' Gwendolyn said frostily.

He looked like a street kid. Seventeen, eighteen? A wolfish grin. What the HELL was he doing in her garden? What happened to the security –

'Hello, Gwendolyn.'

That familiar voice. Cultured. Predatory. Rasping. An old man's voice in the body of a beautiful young boy. And then she recognised him.

'How is this possible?' she whispered. In six months she had struggled to diminish her physical age from eighty-eight to somewhere in her early forties. Yet even so, she still had crow's feet. She still had the vestige of that liver spot. But he, the bastard, had lost seventy years overnight.

'Fresh blood,' admitted Rothbury. 'Acts faster.'

'You said it was dangerous,' Gwendolyn said angrily.

'For the neophyte, yes.'

He was eyeing her up, in that way he used to.

'It doesn't feel right. You look like my grandchild.'

'We don't have a grandchild. I am in fact the grandson of Lord Rothbury's younger brother George. Hence you are my Great Aunt.'

Ah.

Gwendolyn had always been quick on the uptake.

'When is the funeral?'

'Next Sunday.'

'And when do I die?'

'Tonight. You can hardly attend my funeral looking like *that.*'

She always thought she would be the one to die first. It gave her a peculiar satisfaction to have outlasted him.

'And then the great nephew inherits the land and the money and, I assume, also the title,' she said calmly.

'You are looking,' said Rothbury, in his familiar rasp, 'at the 10th Earl of Rothbury.'

'And what should I call him? You?'
'Timothy. Call me Tim.'
Gwendolyn took a deep breath.
I can endure this.
'Hello, Tim.'

YOU ARE NOT ALONE.

Ten of our friends have died in West Drayton.

Six of our friends from Birmingham were arrested at dawn today and have been detained At Our Defenders' Pleasure.

Forty-three of our friends in Aberystwyth took their own lives today by means which we do not wish to describe. It is believed they were expecting imminent arrest and detention.

Attached is the list of the governing body of the society known as the Knight Defenders of Humanity, which we understand became in the twelfth century an offshoot of the society known as the Poor Fellow-Soldiers of Christ and of the Order of Solomon, also known as the Order of the Knights Templar.

YOU ARE NOT ALONE.

You are in danger. All of you, all across the world. You must unite. You must defend yourselves. You must if necessary use guns to defend yourself against those who are trying to either kill you, or enslave you and bleed you against your will.

Attached is a list of places in the United Kingdom where you may obtain hand guns, submachine guns, and grenades by typing in a passcode which will be published on this darknet page at midnight tonight.

YOU ARE NOT ALONE.

Cheyney finished typing.
'Are you sure about this?' asked Harry Barraclough.
'I'm sure.'
He opened another exercise book. Carefully perused the elegant copperplate notations. 'Here is information that may be of interest to the Lothian nest.'

YOU ARE NOT ALONE.

Gwendolyn could not believe the evidence of her eyes. It was monstrous. It was barbaric. It was – it was –

Old blood makes you live forever. But new blood, that's a different kind of buzz entirely. So Jane Carter had said...

Your husband likes it fresh. Sometimes he stabs my breasts and drinks from me as if he was my baby.

There is still juice in this flesh. Or so your husband tells me.

After Jane's cruel hints, which had lingered darkly with her, and after Rothbury's casual admission that he had been drinking *fresh* blood, Gwendolyn had decided she had to know the truth.

I have always loved you, Hugh, in my own way.

And so, while her husband was away in London on business, she installed concealed cameras in the dungeons, embedded into the crevices of the stone pillars.

It took a while but she had always been practically minded.

And I always thought you loved me too. Did you not? Was there not a true bond of love and loyalty between us?

Forgive me, my dear, I noticed you standing there in a reflective mood, may I presume to introduce myself? I am your humble servant, Hugh Rothbury.

She remembered him well, that gallant youth who had stolen her heart.

And you, madam. In a room full of ghastly young women and their ghastly mothers, you are a ray of sunshine. You have a mind, madam, as well as looks and charm. You are – I am lost for words – you are – yes there is only one *bon mot* for this occasion –

And she could now see the same youth, a half century later, in a series of stark medium shots that spanned the entire dungeon, acquiring fresh blood. The fresh blood that allowed him to transmute from geriatric to youngster in the space of a day. The fresh blood he would continue to need to keep his body young and active and soft and unblemished.

She could also see the effect the fresh blood had on him. It inflamed him. It made him crazy with desire. In a dungeon full of slaves, he was no longer the courteous medieval knight. He was a demon filled with lust.

She could not watch for long.

Yes, I have it – You are the belle of this ball, madam! A veritable princess. Now may we dance?

It took them two weeks to get to Rothbury Castle, in a hire car that zigged and zagged along B roads.

Billy had bought a crossbow, the only weapon he could legally purchase. Hayley had acquired a pair of high-powered binoculars and an assortment of knives. They parked the car three miles from the castle and hiked the rest of the way.

On the brow of a small hill they were able to look across to the castle on its summit. The turrets, the crenellations, the drawbridge. With the aid of the scopes Hayley could see men patrolling the parapets, armed with machine guns. Every now and then a helicopter did an aerial patrol of the area. All approaches to the castle were exposed and Hayley guessed they had an arsenal of high-grade weaponry inside.

Rothbury Castle was impregnable.

'Can you still do the thing with the blood?' Billy asked.

'I don't know. I only did it – in anger.'

'Me too.'

What did you expect? That it would be easy?

'What do we do?'

Hayley coughed; that frog in the throat feeling. The skin on her neck fluttered. Her Morpho butterfly tattoo shimmered. Then it detached itself from the soft space below her jaw. It fluttered in the air before them. A bright flash of two-dimensional blueness.

Hayley slowly slumped, then fell asleep. Billy gently lay her down on her back. He cradled her with one arm. He stroked her hair with his hand. He stifled an urge to read her a story.

The Morpho flew from smaller hill to larger hill and entered the castle from above.

In the dungeons, Jane Carter smelled kindred outside the castle. Her weary body twitched. She had no more than a few fluid ounces of blood in her veins. She felt like dust that has been desiccated. Yet still she was able to smell kindred.

Not just kindred. *Her* kindred!

Two days had passed since Gwendolyn had viewed the CCTV footage of Hugh feasting in the dungeons. The trauma of it had, some might argue, unhinged her. And yet she had never felt saner.

Now, in the library, Gwendolyn caressed her husband's head.

You are the belle of this ball, madam! A veritable princess. Now may we dance?

Oh Hugh.

There was a faint down upon his cheeks, the pathetic beginnings of a beard, on a young man barely old enough to grow one. His eyebrows were unruly and black, she remembered how much she had loved that. The head was empty of blood now and she cradled it like, or so she fondly imagined, Judith with Holofernes, in the moments prior to the arrival of her servant bearing a helpful sack.

Rothbury, bless him, had not been expecting it. Surprise was her chief weapon, she had been aware of that. So she had taken down his Crusader dagger from the wall – not the sword, she could barely lift that. And she had checked the sharpness and had spilled a thumb's worth of blood in doing so. And then she had called him on her mobile phone and told him that tea was served in the parlour – oh and by the way she had made some scones. When he entered the room she was behind the door and she struck.

He'd fought her bravely, in fairness. Even with a severed artery in his neck he was still nimble and strong, and he'd struck her arm and knocked the blade out of her grip. And he had grabbed her by the throat and attempted to strangle her with a single hand.

But arterial blood is the elixir of life itself. And as his blood pumped out of him, so his strength pumped out of him, and his grip weakened, and she waited patiently with a cracked trachea. She was drenched in his spray by the end but she continued staring into his eyes until he realised why she was doing this.

Then his grip waned and he fell to the ground. And then, for about forty minutes, she had hacked at his throat until the head was separated from the body.

I gave you my heart, my darling Hugh. What a fool I was, and am. I should have known. You always were a cold and selfish man. But I chose not to see that. Ah, to hell with you, and to hell with me too!

The images of what he had done with those helpless girls would never leave her. The cowardice of his acts appalled her.

But guilt was her true motive. It was not until she had seen Rothbury defiling Jane and Sheila and Sylvia and Tallulah and Una and Sylvestra and all the others, sucking blood and slashing flesh and abusing them in every conceivable way, it was not until then that Gwendolyn's own culpability smote her. Once she had been a girl who was brimming with ideals, a

radical feminist no less by the standards of her age. And now she was –
what?

She had purchased immortality and youth at the cost of, well, her soul.

Gwendolyn excoriated herself for her complete lack of morality. She
did not excuse herself one jot. She did not for a second delude herself that
it was all 'his' fault. She had chosen sin and sin had consumed her.

I am unworthy. I am ashamed. I have transgressed.

When Henderson entered, Gwendolyn was sipping a glass of port.
Rothbury's head was resting now on the coffee table, peering across at the
bookcase. Gwendolyn had wiped her face a little but she still resembled a
blood clot. She beamed at her butler when he entered.

Henderson was fast. He had his gun in his hand and he was
sidestepping nimbly as he took aim. At the same time he was calling into
his throat mic: 'Eagle Down, all units to the parlour, Eagle Down, Out.'
And he was staring at her with shock.

'The tea is cold, Henderson,' she informed him. 'I'll take a fresh pot.'

'Who are you working for?' he whispered, and she actually laughed.

Jane began to sing. The others in her dungeon, with bodies like skeletons,
chained to walls, joined her in her song. A song of hope, or so some
scholars argue; hope slowly blossoming in the darkest days of American
history, when the Underground Railway was a dream that could only be
referred to in allegory:

'Swing low, sweet chariot
Coming for to carry me home.
Swing low, sweet chariot
Coming for to carry me home.'

Morpho flew through the castle courtyard and into the house itself, via
the thin crack between the front door and the frame.

It flapped through the corridor, and into the living room, then through
to the kitchen. It came out again and flew to the library where it found a
scene of carnage, with a headless corpse on the floor and a woman in
handcuffs, held at gunpoint by a dozen or so armed men. There was much
screaming but the woman was strangely calm.

Hayley, who was seeing all this through her butterfly-eyes, wondered
who the woman was and who the dead man was. He looked far too young
to be Rothbury, the owner of the castle.

Morpho flapped onwards. Hayley/Morpho could sense kindred here, somewhere. But it was hard to tell where. Eventually she found a gap in the floorboards and slipped through.

And then downwards further, through another gap in the lower set of floorboards. The scent of kindred was getting stronger.

Morpho/Hayley could hear far-off singing. Sing Low, Sweet Chariot, the old rugby song.

When Morpho flew out of the ceiling and into the dungeon the butterfly beheld the scene and Hayley's spirits sank. Everything she saw appalled her.

It was a vision worse than Hell. Could humans truly do such things?

But despite the anguish of the chained captives, and the stench of bodies, and the bleak horror of these emaciated forms, the slow rhythmic singing shone a glimmer of hope into a scene of dark despair.

Morpho flickered past the prisoners, nothing but skeletons in chains, and Hayley felt rage at the sight of all the decanted blood in glass containers.

Then she saw Jane Carter, with her raven black hair, and a motionless face. Singing lustily. Frail as gossamer. Chained, like all the others, to the walls. Morpho flapped in front of her but Jane didn't comprehend what the little creature was. She didn't know it was a wisp of Hayley, a sliver of her self; and it was too flimsy to bear the scent of kindred.

Morpho flapped against Jane's chains, helplessly. Could she break them? Hayley wondered. Clearly not. Was there a way she could use the butterfly to pick the locks? The very idea was absurd.

'Sing low!' sang the prisoners. One of the old men had a lusty bass voice. Jane had a mezzo soprano. It was very touching. Hayley had no idea what the lyrics meant but she knew it was a spiritual, and the river Jordan was mentioned in the chorus, which stirred her heart strangely.

On the hill that looked across at the Victorian castle set upon the summit of a higher hill, Billy watched Hayley twist and mutter in her sleep.

Brave, he marvelled. *So bloody brave!*

Morpho flapped uselessly against chains, and against the walls, and against the locks, as the lyrics repeated, and repeated:

'I looked over Jordan and what did I see?

Coming for to carry me home.'

Morpho flapped closer to Jane's face, and danced upon her cheeks.

And finally Jane realised what this strange moth-like creature actually was. It was a flying, living *tattoo*. She opened her mouth in astonishment.

Morpho flew inside.

And so Hayley was also inside her now. Inside her own mother. In her mouth, her throat, her stomach. Morpho was so impossibly thin it could pass through flesh so Hayley was in her mother's heart, in her lungs, in her kidneys.

Hayley sensed the creature that was her mother and she marvelled at it. Billy had told her about the two selves theory, the two in one notion. The parasite not-mind and the human-mind, existing in ugly juxtaposition in a single body

But Hayley saw and felt none of that in Jane. Instead, she felt a unity. A single creature.

Mother?

Not Exter, not Human, but a union of the two.

Daughter?

That was how Jane Carter had been able to defy her destiny. The two minds inside her had become one: Exter-Human. A new species; a new life-form.

My name is Hayley. This is pretty embarrassing, I guess. I'm the one who –

None of that matters. Hello Hayley. I am Ursula. That is my real name.

Billy told me. About how –

The plague pit, yes.

You found him –

I ran through the streets.

You kissed him.

We were so in love.

You still are.

You can feel that?

I can feel – everything. A lot.

Don't look too close. Too many dark memories.

I'm going to try something. Open yourself up. Let me be you.

Hayley groaned and twitched and turned – and she gave her life spirit to Morpho.

Ahhh!

Morpho burned with the energies of Hayley's soul. The little butterfly-of-ink-and-skin drank in the power of Hayley's blood and she fed it all to Jane Carter.

And mother and daughter were as one. Their souls touched.

Jane sighed, and gasped, and her power grew. And her chains became taut as her muscles swelled. And she yanked at them. And again. And the stone of the wall cracked and the securing link broke away. And now Jane Carter's arm was free. Then the other arm. Then her legs.

Jane shook the chains off and staggered forward and tottered like a heron on dry land. And then she picked up the vial and unscrewed the top and she drank her own blood, in a series of slow gulps.

And inside Jane's body, Morpho bathed in ecstasy as the blood gouted down into Jane's organs and veins and arteries.

Then Morpho was spat out and Jane howled with joy. And Hayley, through the eyes of Morpho, saw it all. She saw Jane, now free, smashing chains, punching apart stone blocks, liberating her fellow captives.

I did this. I did this! I gave freedom to my kindred! Hayley thought with glee.

And as the chains shattered, the chorus of slaves continued their rousing hope-filled song:

'If you get there before I do

(Coming for to carry me home).

Tell all my friends that I'm coming there too.

(Coming for to carry me home).

About the Author

Philip Palmer is a novelist, screenwriter, and radio dramatist.

He has written five science fiction novels for Orbit Books – *Debatable Space, Red Claw, Version 43, Hell Ship* and *Artemis*. These are fast-paced space opera thrillers with a large streak of dark humour running through them, featuring shameless and sardonic anti-heroes and shockingly ruthless villains. His most recent novel is a fantasy crime thriller called *Hell On Earth* – a police procedural with demons in three linked volumes, set in a future London even darker and more diabolical than our own.

Previously, he has worked as a television and movie script editor, and also as a TV development executive, head of development, and head of drama; and for many years was fortunate enough to make his living reading scripts and novels full-time. He currently teaches screenwriting and creative writing at Goldsmiths University.

His TV script writing credits include *Rebus: The Hanging Garden, Heartbeat, The Bill,* and *The Many Lives Of Albert Walker* (nominated for the Gemini Award in 2002).

Philip is also a distinguished BBC Radio dramatist, with plays including *Gin And Rum, The Faerie Queen,* starring Simon Russell Beale and David Oyelowo, *The King's Coiner* starring Ian McDiarmid, *The Art Of Deception* (2 series), *Red And Blue* (3 series) and *Keeping The Wolf Out* starring Leo Bill, Clare Corbett and Andy Linden (3 series). His science fiction thriller *Invasion* was shortlisted for Best Play in the BBC Audio Awards in 2014.

NewCon Press Novellas Set 5: The Alien Among Us

Nomads – Dave Hutchinson

Are there really refugees from another time living among us? And, if so, what dreadful event are they fleeing from? When a high speed car chase leads Police Sergeant Frank Grant to Dronfield Farm, he finds himself the focus of unwanted attention from Internal Affairs and is confronted by questions he's not sure he ever wants to hear answered.

Morpho – Philip Palmer

When the corpse on the mortuary slab sits up and speaks to Hayley, asking for her help, she thinks she's losing her mind. If only it were that simple… Philip Palmer delivers a tense fast-paced tale of a secret society that governs our world from the shadows, of immortality at a terrible price and events that lead to the overthrow of social order.

The Man Who Would Be Kling – Adam Roberts

When two people ask the manager at Kabul Station to take them into the Afghanizone he refuses. What sane person wouldn't? Said to represent alien visitation, the zone is deadly. Nothing works there. Electrical items malfunction or simply blow up. The pair go in anyway, and the biggest surprise is when one of them walks out again. Nobody survives the zone, so how has she?

Macsen Against the Jugger – Simon Morden

Two centuries after the Earth fell to alien machines known as the Visitors, humanity survives in sparse nomadic tribes. Macsen is an adventurer, undertaking hazardous quests to please Hona Loy. Macsen never fails, but this time he is pitted against a deadly Jugger. Can he somehow survive, or will it fall to his faithful companion Laylaw to tell the tale of his noble death?

NewCon Press Novellas

Released in sets of four, each novella is an independent stand-alone story. Each set is linked by shared cover art, split between the books, providing separate covers that link to form a single image greater than the parts.

Set 1: Science Fiction
Novellas by Alastair Reynolds, Simon Morden, Anne Charnock, Neil Williamson.
Cover art by Chris Moore

Set 2: Dark Thrillers
Novellas by Simon Clark, Alison Littlewood, Sarah Lotz, Jay Caselberg.
Cover art by Vincent Sammy

Set 3: The Martian Quartet
Novellas by Jaine Fenn, Eric Brown, Liz Williams, Una McCormack.
Cover art by Jim Burns

Set 4: Strange Tales
Novellas by Gary Gibson, Adam Roberts, Ricardo Pinto, Hal Duncan.
Cover art by Ben Baldwin

Set 5: The Alien Among Us
Novellas by Dave Hutchinson, Philip Palmer, Adam Roberts, Simon Morden.
Cover art by Peter Hollinghurst

Each novella is available separately in paperback or as a limited numbered hardback edition, signed by the author. Each set is available as a strictly limited lettered slipcase set, containing all four of the books as signed dust-jacketed hardbacks and featuring the combined artwork as a wrap-around.

www.newconpress.co.uk

Immanion Press

Purveyors of Speculative Fiction

www.immanion-press.com

Vivia by Tanith Lee

Tanith Lee was writing grimdark fantasy even before it was known as a genre. Gritty, savage and darkly erotic, *Vivia* is one of the author's darkest - and finest - works. Vivia, the neglected daughter of a vicious warlord, discovers strange, lightless caverns deep beneath her father's castle. Here she finds an entity she believes is a living god and, in her loneliness, seeks its favour. After war and disease devastate her father's lands, Vivia is taken captive by the hedonistic Prince Zulgaris and kept as his concubine. In this barbaric land, where life means very little, and the spectre of the plague haunts the alleys and markets of even the greatest city, circumstances can change very quickly. No life is safe, and treachery abounds. Perhaps, in such a brutal world, only remote pitiless creatures like Vivia can survive unscathed. But at what cost? ISBN: 978-1-907737-98-5 £12.99 $16.99

Songs to Earth and Sky edited by Storm Constantine

Six writers explore the eight seasonal festivals of the year, dreaming up new beliefs and customs, new myths, new dehara – the gods of Wraeththu. As different communities develop among Wraeththu, the androgynous race who have inherited a ravaged earth, so fresh legends spring up – or else ghosts from the inception of their kind come back to haunt them. From the silent, snow-heavy forests of Megalithican mountains, through the lush summer fields of Alba Sulh, into the hot, shimmering continent of Olathe, this book explores the Wheel of the Year, bringing its powerful spirits and landscapes to vivid life. Nine brand new tales, including a novella, a novelette and a short story from Storm herself, and stories from *Wendy Darling, Nerine Dorman, Suzanne Gabriel, Fiona Lane* and *E. S. Wynn*. ISBN 978-1-907737-84-8 £11.99 $15.50 pbk

Tanith Lee From Immanion Press

We are committed to republishing Tanith Lee's long out of print or rare to find novels. The *Blood Opera Sequence* is Tanith's unique take on the vampire myth. If the Scarabae family are indeed vampires – and no one knows for sure – you'll find no others like them in literature or on film.

Dark Dance

After her mother's death, Rachaela is stalked by agents of the mysterious Scarabae family. Despite her instincts to keep away from the Scarabae, she ultimately relents and is taken to the rambling, isolated house near the sea, where they live in baroque seclusion. The fading splendour of the house closes around Rachaela like a stifling womb, and she's given no explanation for the ménage of bizarre oldsters, who are like creatures from an earlier age, and certainly not normal. Is there something supernatural to the Scarabae, or are they merely lost in delusion? ISBN 978-1-907737-85-5 pbk £12.99

Personal Darkness

The Scarabae, an unconventional and eccentric family, who might not be entirely human, have been forced to leave their reclusive home in a remote part of England. Some are dead at the hands of a child created through incest with the purpose of repopulating this ageing branch of the family. Rachaela trails listlessly with the survivors of the Scarabae. She is one of them but still can't feel that she is. The Scarabae relocate to London, and roost within a baroque old mansion. Here, they lick their wounds, but bizarrely appear to be growing younger and mysterious deaths begin to mount up in the city. ISBN 978-1-907737-86-2 pbk £12.99

Darkness I

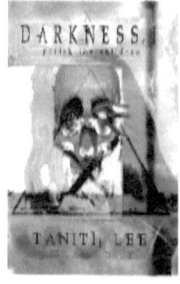

Anna is no ordinary girl. Her parents and the other Scarabae don't know that another member of the family has become aware of her – the father of them all, the almost mythical Cain, who lives apart from the world in a frozen wasteland, where's he's constructed a bizarre reproduction of Ancient Egypt within a pyramid of ice. He wants not only Anna, but other children he believes are reincarnations of people from the past – the earliest times of the family. But what does he want them for? Soon, the kidnappings begin... ISBN 978-1-907737-95-4 pbk £12.99

www.immanion-press.com

www.ingramcontent.com/pod-product-compliance
Lightning Source LLC
Chambersburg PA
CBHW020744130626

46554CB00006B/2146